The Clause

A Tess and Tilly Mystery

by

Kathi Daley

This book is a work of fiction. Names, characters, places, and incidents either are products of the author's imagination or are used fictitiously. Any resemblance to actual events or locales or persons, living or dead, is entirely coincidental.

Copyright © 2019 by Katherine Daley

Version 1.0

All rights reserved, including the right of reproduction in whole or in part in any form.

A Tess and Tilly Cozy Mystery

The Christmas Letter
The Valentine Mystery
The Mother's Day Mishap
The Halloween House
The Thanksgiving Trip
The Saint Paddy's Promise
The Halloween Haunting
The Christmas Clause
The Puppy Project

Chapter 1

Friday, December 6

At what point does a concerned bystander become a stalker?

I'd been asking myself that a lot lately. I'd first met Star Moonwalker six weeks ago when I'd stopped by her antique store during my route as a US Postal Service carrier to deliver a certified letter. After a brief discussion, in which the woman revealed to me that she'd first moved to White Eagle to search for her birth parents, I'd discovered that she was most likely my half sister. I'd also discovered that a man I suspected could be my father very well might have killed the man she'd hired to track down her biological parents, a private investigator named Sam Denton.

Of course, my father being the killer, was not the only explanation. It was also possible that the same people who were after my father, forcing him to fake his own death fifteen years ago, had killed Sam

Denton. Either way, I suspected that Star might be in danger because she had continued to dig around in my father's past even after Denton's death, so I'd been keeping an eye on her, hence the stalking.

Not that Star had been aware that I'd been watching her or digging into her past. I'd been very covert in my approach. I'd started by having my boyfriend, Tony Marconi, do a very quiet computer search into her history, while I began spending time in the woman's antique store, trying to get to know her better. I still didn't know everything I needed to about the events that occurred at the time of Star's birth, so I'd been unable to determine conclusively that she and I shared the same biological father, but it did appear as if my father had been traveling with Star's mother at the time immediately preceding her birth.

"Tess Thomas?" the woman on the other end of the phone line asked.

"Yes, this is Tess." I'd been sitting in my car on hold for a good fifteen minutes, waiting to hear the results of the DNA tests I'd mailed away several weeks before.

"The two samples that you sent do not indicate a familial link."

I narrowed my eyes. "So, the individuals who supplied the two samples are not related?"

"The genetic profiles of the individuals providing the samples demonstrate that it is statistically unlikely a blood relationship exists. A detailed report will be sent to the address you provided within a week. Is there anything else I can help you with?"

"No. Thank you." I hung up and then turned and looked at my dog, Tilly, who'd been waiting patiently. "Well, what do you know about that?"

Tilly shoved her nose into my lap. I looked back toward the house where I'd discovered Star lived. I'd been so certain that she was my half sister that I'd actually dug through her garbage to retrieve a piece of chewing gum I'd seen her throw away to gain a sample of her DNA that I could have compared to my own. At that time, I'd thought the DNA test would simply serve as a confirmation of what I was sure I already knew. How could I have been so wrong?

I focused on the colorful Christmas lights Star had hung along the eaves and around the door and windows as the interior light in a downstairs room went off. A half minute later, a light in one of the upstairs rooms went on. I'd decided the room on the second story at the front of the house must be some sort of workroom or office. Star spent a lot of time in that room when she was home. I slowly stroked Tilly's head as I watched a shadow move across the room. I supposed I really should go before someone noticed me sitting out here. I'd been so sure that Star was my half sister that I'd never even stopped to consider an alternate explanation as to what had occurred when she'd been abandoned by a man I was sure was my father.

I pulled my seat belt across my chest but hesitated to start the engine. The snow that had been threatening all day had begun to fall. I knew I should head home, yet I hesitated. I certainly didn't know everything there was to know about Star's past, but what I did had seemed to support my sister theory. Three years ago, after her adoptive parents passed away, Star had hired Denton to find her birth parents. Through his research, the private investigator found evidence that suggested that Star had been surrendered to a church when she was just hours old. He'd followed up on this evidence and was able to confirm that a man had left the baby with a nun after informing her that the baby's mother had died and she needed a home. The nun had tried to get additional information about the baby and her parents from the man, but he'd refused to answer any questions. Once the baby was safely in the nun's arms, he left. Star had been adopted by wonderful parents and hadn't looked back until after they died.

During his investigation, Denton found out that on the same day Star had been dropped off at the church in Great Falls, Montana, a woman was found shot to death in Buffalo, Wyoming. It was noted in the police report filed after her death that the victim had recently given birth. The detective in charge of the murder case looked for the baby in Wyoming, but the infant was never found. For reasons unknown to me, the investigator did not look for the baby outside that state, so the link to Star was never discovered.

That is until Denton came along and put two and two together. After Star realized that the woman who was shot was most likely her biological mother and that her mother had met with a violent end, she'd decided to give up the idea of searching for answers about her past. She'd paid off the PI and asked him not to look for her father.

A couple of years later, the same PI was asked by a totally different client to find proof that a man who had been living under an alias for years and who everyone believed to be dead, was actually still alive.

During the course of his backtracking to figure out what had really happened to that guy, Denton came across the report filed by the detective who'd been assigned to investigate the murder of the woman who'd been shot in Buffalo just prior to Star being left at the church in Great Falls. Denton immediately realized that the woman mentioned in the report was the same one he believed was Star's mother, and that was when it occurred to me that the man Denton had been hired to find could be my father.

That was confirmed in my mind when Star told me that the owner of the apartment building her biological mother had been staying in when she was shot had identified the man traveling with her was the same man who had dropped off the baby at the church. Star had a copy of the driver's license of that man, and the photo on it was that of a young Grant Thomas, my father, though the name on the license was Grant Tucker, a name Tony and I already suspected he'd used as an alias at one point in his life.

"So Grant Tucker, aka Grant Thomas, was traveling with Star's biological mother but was not her biological father. Why?" I asked Tilly.

She licked my cheek in reply.

I looked down when my phone dinged, indicating I had a text. It was from Tony, wondering what time I'd be home for dinner. I texted back, letting him know I'd had a stop to make but would be home shortly. Once that was accomplished, I turned my attention back to Tilly.

"I suppose it is possible that Star's mother was in some sort of trouble and was on the run from whoever shot her." I let that idea roll around in my mind a bit. "I also suppose that Dad could have been with her to help her escape. Maybe he was a friend of Star's biological mother, or maybe he was some sort of bodyguard." I'd suspected for a while that my dad might work, or at least have worked in the past, for some sort of government agency, such as the CIA.

I hated to think that my father had killed Denton, but he had gone to a lot of trouble to disappear fifteen years ago, and the PI had done a heck of a good job tracking him down. Denton had even managed to provide recent photos of my dad for the man who'd hired him. I knew my dad would not have taken kindly to that.

When Tony and I had tried to track Dad down, we'd met with a ton of resistance, culminating in his rare appearance to tell me to back off. As I thought back on that encounter, I had to admit that he'd seemed more scared than angry. He'd told me that not only had my search put him in danger, but it also put Mom, my brother, Mike, and me in danger as well. I still had no idea why Dad needed to appear to be dead, but I'd been researching him for long enough to know that the people around him tended to die, so maybe he'd been justified in his concern.

Tilly put a paw on my lap, and I looked into her big brown eyes. It was late, and the snow was starting to come down harder. I knew we should head home before Tony began to worry about us. I put my hand on the ignition as a dark blue sedan pulled into Star's driveway. A tall man, dressed casually in a black leather jacket and denim pants, got out and headed to the front door. I realized that Star might have a date. I didn't recognize the guy, but I couldn't really see his face; the sun set early at this time of the year, so even though it was only around six o'clock, it was already pitch dark. I decided to wait to start my vehicle because I didn't want to draw attention to myself. I figured the man would either go inside or Star would come out, and they'd leave together. I watched as the front porch light went on. Star opened the door, said something, and then fell to the ground. Immediately afterward, the man returned to his car and drove off.

"Did that man just shoot Star?" I asked Tilly. I opened my car door just as the vehicle that had been parked in Star's drive pulled away. I ran across the street toward the still-open front door. Star lay lifeless across the threshold. "Oh, God." I pulled out my cell and called Mike, who in addition to being my brother was also a cop. "There's been a shooting," I informed him. "It's Star Moonwalker." I provided the address and told him to hurry.

Mike instructed me to stay put, so I did. I could see that Star was dead, but I felt for a pulse just to be sure, then I called Tilly and walked away from the body. I didn't want to leave Star alone, but I knew better than to do anything to contaminate the crime scene, so I walked toward the far end of the porch and sat down.

In that moment, I wasn't sure what to do. What to feel. On the one hand, until minutes before she'd been shot, I'd believed Star to be my half sister, which had created a false sense of connection between us. On the other hand, I'd only met her about six weeks earlier and didn't know her all that well. I supposed that once the shock wore off, I'd be able to sort out my mixed emotions. Right now, profound grief was all tied up with fear, disbelief, and, most of all, anger. Someone had killed an innocent woman whose seemingly only crime had been curiosity about her birth parents. Star had been a nice woman with a natural presence, a calm manner, and a casual style, reminiscent of the flower children of the 1960s. There certainly didn't seem as if anything could be gained by killing her, and yet someone had.

Despite the fact that I'd been too far away to get a good look at the man who'd pulled up, rung the doorbell, and killed Star, I was pretty sure it had not been my father. This man was tall, as was my father, but my dad had broad shoulders, and this man had appeared to be so thin as to be described as wiry. Of course, the fact that my father had most likely not been the gunman himself didn't mean this man hadn't been hired to do it by the man I'd once called Dad.

I let my mind drift to the man I now think of as a ghost. Grant Thomas was officially deceased, so while that meant he no longer lived, he wasn't really dead either. Prior to Tony uncovering a photo of my father taken three years after his supposed death, I honestly believed that he'd been killed in a truck accident when I was fourteen. I'm not sure why my mind hadn't accepted the fact that my father was dead, but there had always been a part of me that fantasized that the man who was burned so badly as to be unidentifiable was not actually the same man I knew as my father. Tony, being the genius he was even back then, agreed to dig around. It had taken him twelve years to find the photo, but once he had proof of life after the accident, I'd grabbed onto the mystery and hadn't let go of it since. Of course, the more I dug, the more I learned and the more disturbed I became.

I watched as Mike pulled up along the street in front of the house. He headed up the front steps, knelt down in front of the body to check for a pulse, and then looked in my direction. "Are you okay?"

I nodded.

"What happened?"

I hesitated. I couldn't very well tell my brother that I'd been watching this woman from across the street without going into a lot more explanation than I was willing to at this point, so I told him that I'd been driving by, heard a gunshot, saw a blue sedan pull away from the house, and had gone to check it out, which is when I saw the woman stretched out dead across the threshold.

"Did you know this woman?" Mike asked.

"Sort of. As I said, her name is Star Moonwalker. She owns an antique store in town. I deliver mail to her sometimes, and when I have time, I stop in and look around while I am there. We chat while I look, so in a way, you could say we knew each other."

Mike took out his handheld radio and spoke to Frank Hudson, his second in command. He confirmed that the coroner was on the way, and then he returned his attention to me. "I need to process the scene and see to the removal of the body. I am going to want to ask you some additional questions. If you'd like, I can come by your cabin to talk to you when I'm done here."

I nodded. "Okay. That sounds good. It is getting pretty cold."

"Can you describe the person who drove away from the scene?"

"Male. Tall. Black leather jacket, denim pants. It was dark, so I didn't see his face."

"And the car?"

"A blue sedan. A Ford, I think, but I'm not sure. I do know it was one of those midsize sedans. I didn't notice the license plate, I'm afraid. The whole thing happened so fast that it seems it was over before I knew to pay attention."

"And you were just driving by?" Mike asked.

I glanced at the ground and nodded. I could see that Mike didn't believe me, and I knew he wasn't going to let this go, but Frank pulled up just then, so Mike walked Tilly and me back across the street to my Jeep. He opened the door, and Tilly jumped up. I slid in after her.

"I'll be by when I can. In the meantime, I want you to write down everything you can remember," Mike instructed through the open driver's side window as I adjusted my seat belt.

"Okay."

"And Tess—"

I took a chance and looked him in the eye. "Yeah?"

"When I come by, I'm going to want the rest of the story."

I swallowed and nodded. He kissed me on the cheek and then stepped away. He closed the door, and I started the ignition and pulled away.

Mike knew that Dad was still alive. I'd finally broken down and told him a year ago. But he didn't know the rest. The part I'd been keeping from him. I wasn't exactly sure how he'd react, but I knew him well enough to know he wasn't going to be happy about any of it. I supposed I knew that one day I'd have to confess everything; I just hadn't realized when I'd left work for the weekend that that day was today.

As I drove toward the cabin where Tony, his dog, Titan, and my cats, Tang and Tinder, were waiting, I felt my stress level increase dramatically. I supposed it might be the result of delayed reaction from the shooting, but I supposed it could also have been heightened by my impending conversation with Mike. I knew it was going to be unpleasant. The truth of the matter was that I'd known our dad was alive a full year before I'd even brought Mike in on the secret. Mike was a good guy, and I trusted him implicitly, but he was also pretty intense. He tended to act before thinking when it came to protecting the people he loved, so I rightfully feared he'd only make things worse if he knew our father was still alive and kicking in the world.

Of course, even after I'd shared with Mike the proof Tony and I had found of the existence of the man we both thought had died years before, I hadn't continued to fill him in on every little detail of our investigation as I'd promised I would. I hadn't told him that Dad had shown up at the hospital when Mike was shot and had almost died, and I hadn't told him about Star or the suspicion I'd had that she was our half sister. Though my suspicion had turned out to be wrong, our dad had been involved with her mother in some way. I was sure he'd been the one to drop her off at the church, so whether he was her father or not, he'd been connected to her from the beginning.

Deep in my heart, I was sure that it was this connection that had led to her death. Maybe I should have done more to warn her that digging around in the past of Grant Thomas, or Grant Tucker as it might be, could only lead to trouble for everyone involved. Maybe instead of watching her from afar, I should have confronted her about the envelope I'd delivered to her when we first met. An envelope she'd told me contained a copy of the file Sam Denton had built on the man I was certain was my father. Denton must have known his life was in danger because he'd given a copy of his file to a friend for safekeeping. The friend knew about Star's situation and had decided to send it to her after Denton's death.

I turned onto the narrow road leading to my cabin. The file had concerned me from the beginning, but Star had assured me that she'd locked it away in her safety deposit box. She'd told me she hadn't read it after she'd opened it in my presence on the day I delivered it and had no idea what was in it. I didn't know what sort of evidence Denton had managed to dig up, but apparently, it was damaging enough to cause someone to decide to end the life of both the PI who'd built the file and the woman who'd currently been in possession of it.

Chapter 2

"Are you okay?" Tony asked when Tilly and I arrived at the cabin.

I guess he must have heard about the shooting from Mike, or perhaps Mike's wife, my best friend, Bree, had called him because he seemed to know exactly what was going on before I filled him in.

I nodded. I knew I should say something more, but my throat felt tight, and I was sure the tears would begin to flow if I didn't do everything in my power to hold them at bay.

Tony opened his arms, and I stepped into them. He held me for a moment before he spoke. "I was going to suggest we pick up dinner on the way out to my place, but I guess we should wait here for Mike. How about an omelet?"

"An omelet sounds good," I answered, tightening my hold around his waist. I took a deep breath and stepped back just a bit. "I'm going to change out of my uniform, and then we can talk."

"Okay," Tony said. "I'm going to feed the animals while you do that."

I kissed him quickly on the cheek and then headed into the bedroom, where I slipped into a pair of jeans and a pale blue sweatshirt. I pulled my long hair off my face, secured it with a band, slipped on a pair of thick wool socks, and headed back to the kitchen. I found Tony cracking eggs into a bowl.

"Do you want cheese in your omelet?" he asked.

"Yes, please. And olives and tomatoes if we have them."

"We do." Tony crossed the room to the refrigerator. "Mushrooms?"

"Sure, why not?"

He took out a knife and cutting board and began to slice the vegetables.

"I'm sorry I didn't tell you that I was sitting in front of Star's house when you texted," I said, jumping right in. "I'm not sure why I didn't tell you, but the truth of the matter is that I've spent quite a lot of time watching her lately. I guess I knew it was wrong. Creepy, even. So when you asked, I lied about what I was doing."

"Why were you watching her?" Tony asked as he began dicing a tomato.

I blew out a breath. Why *had* I been watching her? "I guess after she told me what she had found out about her birth parents, and I realized that she might very well be my half sister, I was pretty messed up. I was angry and jealous, which made me slightly obsessed, but most of all, I was worried."

Tony stopped what he was doing and looked at me. "We did talk about the fact that knowing about your father's past might put her in danger, so I understand being worried, but jealous?"

"I know this is going to sound crazy, and I feel like I literally might be crazy for even feeling this way, but it really bothered me that my dad might have had a child before Mike and me."

Tony returned to his dicing. "I guess I understand that."

"And not only was I jealous that Dad might have had a daughter before he had us, but I was really upset that he'd abandoned her. I know none of this makes sense, but I guess the knowledge that Dad abandoned Star when she needed him most played into my own feelings of abandonment after finding out that he faked his own death and left Mike and Mom and me to fend for ourselves."

Tony handed me a glass of wine, but he didn't respond.

"Add to that the fact that I knew that looking for my father could put Star in danger, and I found myself obsessing over her actions, her whereabouts, her safety. Really, every little aspect of her life," I continued.

Tony turned on the stove and slipped a pat of butter into a heavy pan. "So, you began stalking her."

I nodded. "Yes, I guess I did." I could see he was hurt that I'd kept that piece of information even from him. I supposed I didn't blame him. He'd helped me every step of the way and had never once seemed judgmental. "I not only began stalking her, I actually dug gum from her trash and had her DNA compared to mine."

"And?"

"And we aren't sisters."

Tony raised a brow. "Really. I have to admit that I was pretty much convinced you were after everything we've discussed in the past."

"I'm still convinced that it was my father who surrendered her to the church, but I suppose there must have been a different reason why he was traveling with Star's mother when she was born. Maybe they were friends, or maybe he was supposed to protect her from whoever shot her. I'm not sure we'll ever know the answer to that question unless, of course, it is contained in the report that Star stashed away for safekeeping."

Tony poured the eggs into the preheated pan.

"I'm sorry I didn't tell you I'd been watching her, and I'm sorry I didn't tell you about the DNA test I requested," I added. "I had no reason to keep either from you. I don't even know why I did."

"I'm not mad," He began layering in the cheese and veggies. "I understand how hard this whole thing has been on you, and it does appear that you were right to be concerned for Star's safety."

"So you agree with me that her death is most likely related to the fact that she was digging around in her past?"

Tony crossed the room and opened the refrigerator. He pulled out a carton of grated Parmesan. "I do think that her digging around might have led to her death, but there are a lot of other reasons someone might have wanted her dead as well."

"Like what?"

"Maybe she was shot by a scorned lover or an old business partner. Maybe the shooter was after the same antique clock she was bidding on and wanted her out of the way. I know the odds are that she was indeed killed because of her research into her past, but I think it might be a mistake to focus exclusively on that as a motive and not to at least consider other options."

I shrugged as I picked a petal from one of the red carnations on the table. "I guess it is possible that there could be other reasons that some mysterious guy would simply pull up in front of Star's house and shoot her while she stood helplessly in the doorway. I'm sure Mike will be all over the various possibilities once he has a chance to catch his breath."

"I suppose we can talk to him about it when he stops by."

"If he doesn't kill me for not telling him what I now realize I am going to need to share with him if he is to have all the information he needs to conduct a thorough investigation." I groaned. "He is going to be so mad."

Tony set the salt, pepper, and Parmesan on the table. "I agree that he is going to be mad, but he is also going to be hurt. I guess you should be prepared for the full spectrum of emotions when he finds out you've been lying to him."

Leaning forward, I rested my head on my arms. "I know. And I do feel bad that I've been keeping things from him, but if I'm perfectly honest, I'm not sure I would do things any differently even if I could go back and change things." I sat up and looked at Tony. "Mike was in the hospital clinging to life when Dad came to visit. There was no way I was going to bring him in on what was an emotionally charged encounter at that point. And then, as time went by, it seemed awkward to tell him. And when I found out that Star might be our half sister, I was so stunned I wasn't sure what to do with that information. I knew that the knowledge that we might have a half sister would put Mike over the edge. It put *me* over the edge, and I'm not nearly as reactive as he is. I know I need to tell him now, but I'm really not sorry that I didn't tell him then. I'm sorry that he is going to be hurt by the decisions I made; I'm just not sure they were the wrong decisions to have made at that time."

Tony cut the omelet in half and slid it onto two plates. Then he added toast and handed me one of the plates.

"And your mom. Don't you think this might be a good time to bring her into this? If Star did die because of what she found out about your father, it is eventually going to come out that your father is alive."

I sliced off a piece of egg. "If we have to tell her to ensure her safety, we will, but unless it really becomes an issue, I'd rather not. If she knows Dad is alive and has, in fact, been alive all these years under an alias, it will hurt her deeply. I don't want her to be hurt. Besides, she has been over-the-top stressed out ever since she found out that the event planner for Christmas on Main resigned, leaving her in charge of everything."

Tony topped off both our glasses of wine. "What happened with that anyway?"

"Apparently, the woman they hired to oversee the event got an offer that would pay her more money, so she took advantage of the Christmas Clause, which stated that, due to the high demand for her services over the holiday, she'd be allowed to terminate the contract she had with the committee, as long as she did so two weeks before the event."

"That's crazy. Why would the committee have signed a contract like that in the first place?"

"I guess no one read the fine print. Or if they did read it, they either didn't understand it or weren't concerned that it would become an issue. Either way, the event planner has left town, and Mom and the rest of the committee are scrambling to get everything done."

"I'm sorry to hear that. Maybe we can help."

"I've already volunteered us," I informed the man I loved. "I think we should both plan to be available for the holiday parade next weekend, the carnival, and Christmas on Main the following weekend."

"I'm happy to do what I can." Tilly and Titan both jumped up and ran to the door. "It sounds like Mike is here," Tony announced.

I pushed my half-eaten omelet aside. It was probably best not to have a full stomach as I faced the inquisition I knew was coming.

"It's going to be fine." Tony squeezed my hand as he reached for the door to greet Mike.

I knew it wasn't going to be fine, but I had very few options at that point, so I took a deep breath and prepared myself for the fireworks I knew were inevitable once Mike found out that I'd actually seen and spoken to Dad but had neglected to share that bit of information with him.

Chapter 3

Saturday, December 7

"Rough night?" Tony greeted me with a mug of coffee as I stumbled from the bedroom.

"You know it was. I'm sorry I kept you awake with all my tossing and turning."

"It's okay. I understand completely. Last night was rough. I expected Mike to be mad and even hurt, but I hadn't expected him to be as angry as he was."

I poured a dollop of cream in my coffee and sat down at the counter. "I'm pretty sure he is never going to speak to me again. He wouldn't even listen when I tried to explain why I hadn't told him about Dad's visit and why I'd wanted to be sure Star was our half sister before I brought up that situation."

"I think he feels as if you have treated him like a child. As if you are somehow managing his life by deciding what information he should and should not have access to."

I guess Tony had a point. That was exactly what I had been doing from the first minute I'd found out that our dad hadn't died all those years ago as we'd been told. I supposed that was what I was doing with Mom at this point as well. I really hadn't been trying to hurt Mike, but my attempt to protect my big brother had done just that.

"Should I call him?" I asked.

Tony sat down across from me. "I wouldn't. I think you might want to give him the weekend to get over his anger."

"Yeah, I guess you're right." I took a sip of my coffee. "Though I do feel that we need to act on what happened to Star before the trail goes cold."

"Mike is the cop here," Tony reminded me. "It is his job to find Star's killer."

"I know it is his job, but he doesn't know everything we do. I tried to tell him about Star's mother and her relationship with our father, but I could tell that he stopped listening once I brought up the fact that I'd seen and spoken to Dad but hadn't thought it important to inform him of his visit."

Tony sat quietly for a moment. I suspected he was trying to work things through in his own mind. Finally, he spoke. "Mike is a good cop. Eventually, when he is ready, he'll come to you to get the rest of the story. But I really think we should let him take the lead on this. Before all this happened, we'd planned to go out to my place to cut down a couple of trees. We were going to decorate and generally relax before the holiday events that are coming up for the next two weekends take up all our time. I think we should do that. Mike will call us when he's ready."

I wanted to argue, but I knew Tony was right. Besides, Tony's big computers were out at his place. I was still trying to get my thoughts straight, but I suspected that before the weekend was over, I'd have Tony and his hacker know-how digging for information that might lead us to the person who'd shot and killed an innocent woman for allowing her curiosity to get the better of her.

******

"Is this one too tall for your living room?" I asked Tony as we tramped through the forest with the dogs on our heels.

"It would fit, I think, but it is going to be too heavy for the two of us to carry. The thing must be twenty feet tall, and it's full, with a pretty thick trunk. Perhaps we should either look for something smaller or something closer to the road that we won't have to carry so far."

I supposed Tony had a point. We'd hiked through knee-deep snow up a fairly steep hill to find this tree, but I hadn't stopped to consider the fact that if we found the perfect tree on the hill, we'd need to carry it back through that same knee-deep snow to get it back to the truck.

"Maybe we should have brought a sled," I said. "We could have hooked the dogs up to it and let them pull it down the hill."

"A good suggestion for next year."

I ran my hand over the branches of a tree that was only six feet in height but full and shaped nicely. "This would be a nice one for the cabin."

Tony walked over to where I was standing. He repositioned the ax he held over his shoulder. "I agree; it's a nice tree. Maybe we can get the tall one we saw near the road for my place. It wasn't quite as full as the trees up here on the mountain, but the branches were dispersed evenly, and we won't have to carry it far."

I nodded. "I think that one will be fine for the living room in your house. Let's get a small one for the bedroom as well. It would be pretty to snuggle up in your big bed in front of the fire while the tree lights twinkle and the snow falls outside the window."

Tony leaned over and kissed me gently on the lips. "Now, that sounds just about perfect."

I found myself smiling. "It does sound pretty perfect, doesn't it? In fact, let's get a small one for both bedrooms."

Tony confirmed one more time that this was definitely the tree I wanted for the living room of the cabin, then handed me his backpack while he took the ax to it. By the time we'd lugged the six-foot tree down the snowy hill, I was exhausted and doubly happy that we hadn't decided to try to manage the twenty-foot tree I'd pointed out.

"Should we drop the small trees off at the cabin before we head back to your place?" I asked.

"They will be fine out on the deck. We'll decorate the trees at the lake house this afternoon and then head back to the cabin tomorrow afternoon. We'll pick up a pizza tomorrow to eat while we decorate."

"And tonight?"

"Tonight I have a meatball and pasta soup ready to reheat. I have fresh greens and a loaf of bread from the bakery. It should be an easy meal to assemble when we're ready."

"Sounds perfect."

And it was. I'm not sure how Tony accomplished it, but he managed to get me to forget about Star for one day and enjoy the kickoff to the season. We'd decorated the house, played with the dogs in the snow, shared a wonderful meal by candlelight, and were talking about watching the holiday movie I'd seen advertisements for all week when Mike called to speak to Tony. I think it is important to emphasize that he'd called Tony, not me.

"What'd he want?" I asked after Tony hung up.

"He had some questions about the envelope that you'd told him that Star had in her possession, which seems to have been what started this whole thing."

"Don't you think he should have asked me about the envelope since I was the one to deliver the package to Star in the first place?" I asked with irritation.

"Do you know anything about the envelope other than what you already told him?"

"No," I admitted.

"Then I suppose he figured there wasn't a good enough reason to extend an olive branch to you at this point. He's still pretty mad."

"I know." And I also knew I deserved his anger. "What else did he want from you?"

"He wanted me to see if I can get into any records that Sam Denton may have left anywhere on the internet. Even if he or someone else deleted the files,

I might be able to find traces of what at one time existed."

"Why doesn't he just get a subpoena to access the file Star left in her safety deposit box?"

"He'd need to go through the courts to get access, and that will take time. He hoped I could find something more quickly. I told him I'd head downstairs and work on it now. I'm sorry about the movie. I guess I'll need a rain check."

"That's okay. This is more important. Can I help?"

Tony hesitated and then nodded. "It will help if you can go over the timeline again."

"I can do that. Where do you want me to start?"

"At the beginning, but let's head downstairs first. We can chat while I work."

Once Tony and I got settled in his computer room, he asked me to start by going back over everything I knew about both Star and Sam Denton. I didn't have a specific timeline in that I couldn't confirm actual dates, but I did have a general overview of what had happened.

"As a newborn, Star was left at a church by a man I now believe to have been my father in 1979. A couple named Sonny and Dharma Moonwalker adopted her. After her adoptive parents both passed, she decided to look for her birth parents, so she hired Sam Denton to find them. Sam is the one who found out that Star had been left at the church by a man who declined to identify himself. He also found out that a woman who had recently given birth had been shot and killed at about the same time Star was left at the church."

"So Star originally hired Denton in 2016?" Tony asked.

"That seems about right as far as I know. She wasn't specific about the date when I spoke to her."

Tony typed some commands into the computer. "Okay, go on."

"After Denton told Star about her mother's violent end, she realized she might be better off not knowing all the details of her birth, so she paid Denton off and asked him to stop looking. I don't know when that was exactly, but she made it sound as if he had found out what he knew about her mother in a relatively short amount of time, so that may have taken place two or three years ago. It's hard to say."

"Okay." Tony continued to type. "So she decided to stop her search. Then what?"

"At some point after that, Denton was hired by someone else to find proof that a man everyone believed to be dead was actually alive. I believe that man was my father. Denton found a link between the man he was looking for and the one who'd dropped Star off at the church. Once he confirmed that the two men were most likely one and the same, he contacted Star again."

"And do you know when that was?"

I tried to remember. After a minute, I slowly shook my head. "No. I don't think she said. If she did, I don't recall. I have the feeling, however, that it was recently. Within the past year. All I know for sure is that not only did Denton provide Star with a name and photo of the man who dropped her off at the church, he was also able to photograph the man who was supposed to be dead and provide those photos to his client. Shortly after Denton provided Star with the same photos, she found out that he had been shot and killed."

Tony paused and looked up. "Any idea of the name of the client who hired Denton to find your father?"

I shook my head. "No idea. I don't think Star knew. If she did, she didn't say."

"And you don't know when Denton died?"

"I don't, but Star did tell me that Denton made a copy of his file and left it with a friend. Sometime after Denton's death, his friend sent the file to her. I delivered that file to Star back in October, so I would guess that Denton died a month or two before."

Tony continued to search. "I'm not finding an obituary or any business listings for a private investigator named Sam Denton. Did Star ever mention another name? Maybe a full name or a business title?"

"She never said." I narrowed my gaze. "Wait, I remember something." I paused to dig around in my memory. "Spring. Star said that Denton had tracked down the man he'd been hired to find this past spring. Star said that once Denton provided the proof-of-life photos of the man he'd been looking for to his client, his assignment was complete, and it was at that point he offered to continue looking into the guy for Star because he believed that this man was her father. Star wanted to take a few days to think it over, and it was during that time that Denton was shot and killed."

"So, Denton died this past spring?"

"Yes, I think so. I'm not sure why the file wasn't sent to Star until October if Denton died in the spring, but now that I think about it, I'm sure that is what she told me."

"Okay."

Tony continued to type while I continued to think back to my conversation with Star. Once I realized that the man she was talking about was most likely my father, I think I sort of blacked out and didn't catch the rest of what she'd said. Talk about a shock!

"I think I found something," Tony said. "A man named Adam Samuel Denton was shot and killed in his home in Casper, Wyoming this past May. According to a newspaper article I found, he was a private investigator who lived alone and tended to travel a lot for work. His closest living relative at the time of his death was a cousin who lived in Pittsburg."

I got up and began to pace. "Okay, so Denton was killed in May. I wonder if we have any information regarding what my father was doing then." I paused and continued to walk. "Mike was shot in April, which is when Dad came to White Eagle with a warning for us to back off. And I did. We did. For a while. I guess we'd stopped tracking him by May."

Tony nodded. "I'm afraid that you are correct in that we'd stopped tracking your dad by May and don't have any information about his whereabouts since this past April. I can go back to try to find out where he was in May, but it will take a while."

"Okay. Maybe we'll do that later. What can we determine based on what we know right now?"

"I'm not sure we can say anything with any degree of certainty at this point. It might be best to determine the questions and then look for specific answers."

That sounded reasonable and a whole lot more manageable. "Okay, then I suppose the first thing I'd want to know is why my father was with Star's mother when she died. And who killed her? And why was she killed? Did my dad know she was in trouble and were they running from someone when Star was born or did they just happen to be together when Star's mother was killed?"

"All good questions."

"I'm just getting started." I continued to pace. "I suppose an even more relevant question might be who hired Denton to find my father? And why did he want him found? Did my father kill Denton because he provided photos of his existence to his client? Or did someone who was after my father kill him? Might Denton's client have killed him after he finished his mission? And what did whoever hired a private investigator to find my father do with the information he hired Denton to find once they had it? Is my father in danger? Is he even still alive? Are Mike, my mom, and I in danger? Should we look for Dad or just leave this alone?"

Tony got up. He crossed the room, pulling me into his arms when he reached me. "It's okay. It's all going to be okay. I don't have any answers yet, but I'll find them. And I won't let anything happen to you. I promise. We just need to keep our heads and work on those questions one at a time." He tilted my chin up and looked me in the eye. "Okay?"

I nodded, even though I was feeling far from okay. "Do you think my dad killed Star?"

"Why would your dad do that?"

"She had the information Denton dug up. My dad went to a lot of trouble to disappear. I would think he would be pretty unhappy that Denton took photos of him."

"Your dad probably saved Star's life when she was an infant. He made sure she was in a safe place and would be taken care of before he took off. I doubt he would turn around and kill the woman that baby had become forty years later."

I supposed Tony was correct, but his explanation didn't do a lot to quell the knot in my stomach.

Chapter 4

Monday, December 9

"Morning, Bree," I said to my best friend and sister-in-law as I popped into the bookstore she owned to deliver her mail.

"Hello," she answered politely. "How was your weekend?"

"It was fine," I answered. I hated to admit it, but she sounded almost as peeved with me as Mike was. "Tony and I got our trees cut and set up," I decided to avoid the topic of Star's murder altogether. "We'll have to have you and Mike over for dinner soon so you can see our decorations."

"Maybe," she answered noncommittally.

I leaned my elbows on the counter. Tilly must have realized we were going to be here for a while because she wandered over to the pillow Bree kept for her and laid down. "Are you mad at me too?"

Bree hesitated. She looked conflicted, and then she tightened her lips and crossed her arms over her chest. "Of course, I'm mad at you. How could you do that to Mike? To me? We've been nothing but supportive since you first spilled the beans about your father. I really thought we were all in this thing together. Like a team. But apparently, you are doing what you always do and cutting everyone out."

"I wasn't trying to cut you out," I defended myself.

"Yes, you were," she insisted. "You always do that. And you know why you always do that? Because you think you are better than everyone else. You think that Mike and I, and even Tony, are so weak and inferior that we can't handle the same level of stress as the great Tess Thomas."

Ouch. That really hurt. I wanted to lash back at her, but maybe Bree was right. I did tend to protect those around me by not sharing the more difficult aspects of my life. And I had intentionally decided that Mike couldn't handle the truth about Dad or Star. Had I been wrong? I hadn't thought so at the time, but now that Bree had put everything out on the table, maybe I had felt they weren't equipped to handle the same level of danger and intrigue that I was.

"I'm sorry," I said. "I never meant to hurt you or Mike."

"Maybe not, but you did. Mike has been so good about letting you be involved in his cases even though he doesn't really need your help. He is, after all, the cop, and you are, after all, only the postal carrier. But Mike still lets you in. He respects you enough to entertain your ideas. It would be nice if you would have extended that same consideration to him."

I was pretty sure I physically cringed at that comment. "You're right. And I am sorry. I don't know what more I can say. I didn't mean to hurt Mike, but when my dad showed up, Mike was clinging to life in the hospital. I certainly wasn't going to bring it up then."

"And later? After he recovered?"

I exhaled slowly. "I don't know. I guess it just never seemed like the right time. And you know how Mike would have responded if I'd told him that I suspected that Star was our half sister. There was no way he would have left it alone. I just wanted to be sure before I said anything."

"Has it occurred to you that by not telling Mike what was going on, you might have gotten Star killed?"

It *had* occurred to me. More than once. I picked up my bag, turned, and left the bookstore. I'd need to make things up to Bree at some point but now was not that time. I felt bad enough about my part in Star's death; the last thing I needed was someone reminding me that I'd all but shot the woman myself. If I'd told Mike what I knew right from the beginning, he might have done something better or different, something that would have allowed her to be here with us, celebrating the magic of the Christmas season.

"Let's cross over and do Hattie's next," I said to Tilly. I'd been heading toward Sisters' Diner, the restaurant my mother owned with my aunt, Ruthie, but suddenly, I felt that I was going to be unable to look Mom in the eye. I'd been lying and keeping things from her for years. I'd felt justified for doing so and had convinced myself that it was in her best interest, but was I really just playing the part of the superior being as Bree had just indicated I tended to do? I liked to think I was better than that but was I?

When had life become so darn complicated?

"Morning, Hattie," I said as I entered the bakeshop. I took a deep breath as I took in the cinnamon, vanilla, peppermint, and even pumpkin. "It always smells so good in here. Is that chocolate?"

She nodded. "I have some double fudge cookies in the oven."

"That sounds wonderful. I may have to loop back around later to grab a couple."

"I'll set a couple aside for you once I get them frosted. The chocolate goes well with the house blend of coffee I've been serving if you have time for a break later."

"I'll keep that in mind." I set Hattie's mail on the counter.

"I guess you heard about Star Moonwalker," she said.

I nodded but decided not to point myself out as the one who found find her. "I did hear. I didn't know her well, but she seemed like such a nice woman."

"She was a very nice woman. I can't imagine who would have wanted her dead, although there are theories a plenty floating around town."

"What sort of theories?" I asked.

Hattie shrugged. "There are those who think that Star got mixed up with the wrong guy, and others who think she had some sort of a secret past that finally caught up with her, but most think that she got herself into some sort of a bad business deal that went horribly wrong."

"A bad business deal?"

"I don't have the details, but apparently, Star bought a bunch of furniture at an estate sale, and there are those who suspect she might have had to take on an investor to afford everything she purchased and that the investor turned on her after she tried to cut him out. Personally, I'm not sure any of these theories hold water. I think folks just like to speculate when something like this happens."

"Do you know anything about the estate sale or the rumored investor?" I had to admit that an explanation for Star's murder that didn't involve my father would go a long way toward my peace of mind.

"No. Like I said, rumors are running rampant."

I supposed that was to be expected. "You mentioned a secret past. I don't suppose you have any additional details about that?"

"Not really. Star moved to White Eagle several years ago to look for her birth parents; I do know that. But I asked her about her progress a few times, as have others in the community, and she seemed to have clammed up. It is a bit odd that she started off speaking freely about her search, and then all of a sudden told everyone that she'd changed her mind, and had given up the search. There are a lot of us who think she found out something she wished she hadn't. Like maybe her parents were criminals or something. Of course, there are others in town who think she had rich parents who decided they didn't want a child, so when she found them, they paid her off to keep things quiet."

"Why would they do that?"

Hattie shrugged. "No idea, and as I've said, all of it is speculation. Until the facts relating to Star's murder are made public, folks are going to fill in the blanks with whatever they can come up with."

Hattie might be right about that. I supposed that was how rumors got started. I picked up the mailbag I'd left resting at my feet. "I should get going. I'll stop by later to pick up those cookies you promised me."

"They'll be waiting."

While part of me hoped that Star's death had been the result of a business deal gone bad, I sort of doubted that would be the case. And I found it interesting that one of the theories floating around was of a secret past. Hattie had been off about the rich parent angle, and Star had talked about finding her parents to quite a few folks when she first moved to the area, but I had to wonder if Star hadn't shared something more specific and closer to the truth with someone close to her. I supposed she might have. I mean, I'd just met her when she basically shared the whole story of her past with me.

If Star *had* shared the details of her past with someone in the community, that would be important information to have. Maybe I should ask around to try to figure out who she might have shared her secret with. Maybe I'd ask Hattie about it again when I stopped by to pick up my cookies.

Chapter 5

Tony had called me earlier and left a message, filling me in on the fact that Mike had asked him to run down some phone numbers, so he'd gone out to his house by the lake. He'd taken the animals, other than Tilly, who was with me, out there with him, and asked that I meet him there when I finished work for the day. I normally didn't mind the extra drive, but it had been a really long day, so the message left me feeling grumpier than usual. But the things Bree had said to me, while rough, really had hit home, so I was determined to try to make things up to Tony by setting aside my fatigue and at least appearing to be as happy and pleasant as possible.

When I arrived at his place, I found a note letting me know he was down in his computer room. The place was airtight and soundproof, so I knew calling out wouldn't do any good. I greeted the animals, changed out of my uniform, and headed downstairs.

When I walked into the room, Tony looked up and smiled at me.

"Oh good, you got my message."

"I did. You look busy."

He nodded, pushed back his chair, and stood up. "Mike pulled Star's phone records. There were a few things that stood out that he wanted to follow up on. I'd offered to help, and he decided to take me up on it."

"What sort of things?" I asked as he took my hand and led me out of the room.

"Mostly telephone conversations that Star engaged in during the last couple of weeks of her life. There were several calls to the bank, at least three calls to Austin Wade, several from a woman named Celia Bronson, a bunch to an unlisted number I still need to track down, and quite a few to and from a burner cell."

"And were you able to figure out the content of the calls?"

Tony nodded as we headed into the kitchen. He opened the refrigerator and poked his head inside. "I was able to track down some of the information Mike was after, but not all of it. Apparently, Star was conversing with the bank about a loan she hoped to get to buy a desk and some other furniture from an estate sale. The loan officer was able to verify that her loan had not been approved, but it was his understanding that Star had found a partner and no longer needed the loan anyway."

"Did he know who the partner was?" I asked while reaching for two wine glasses.

"No. Mike is looking in to it."

"And the calls to Austin?" I asked. Austin Wade was a member of one of the founding families of White Eagle, and probably the richest man in the area.

"It seems Star was successful in her bid to buy that desk and wanted to ask him if he could provide some information about it."

I leaned a hip against the counter. "What sort of information?"

Tony pulled out a package of fresh Parmesan, some heavy cream, and a stick of butter. It looked like fettuccine Alfredo was in our future. "Apparently, the desk that she purchased was a very old and very valuable desk from the Colonial era. The craftsman who made it was known for adding secret compartments to his furniture. Star believed her desk contained such a compartment, but she couldn't figure out how to find it. She'd heard from a customer that Austin had a similar desk, so she called him for pointers. I guess they went back and forth a few times, trying to figure out if there was a secret compartment in it, and if there was, where it might be."

"Did she ever find it?"

"Austin didn't know. As of the last time he spoke to her, she hadn't, but that was two days before her death."

The concept of a hidden drawer or compartment in a desk was intriguing. I figured we might want to circle back to that one. "And this Celia Bronson?"

"So far, neither Mike nor I have been able to track her down. I also haven't had any luck with the burner cell, so after a full day of work, we don't have much more than we did when we started our search." Tony opened a bottle of wine, poured it into the glasses I'd taken down, and handed one to me.

"I'm not sure you haven't made progress," I countered. "You might not have found a smoking gun, but I think the fact that Star bought a desk that was so expensive that she considered taking out a loan to pay for it might be relevant. Hattie mentioned something to me today about a rumor that has been floating around. There's speculation that Star's death might have had something to do with a business deal she'd entered into."

Tony filled a pan with water and put it on the stove to heat. He then began grating Parmesan. "Did Hattie have any information specific to the rumor?"

"No," I answered. "It was one of many, but still, it seems as if it might be worth following up on."

Tony melted the butter in the pan. "I know Mike was going to look into it. He also planned to look for the desk Star had purchased. He didn't find it in her home or her store."

"So maybe the partner has it."

"Perhaps."

I took a sip of my wine. "Did you find any other information that might be relevant to the case?"

"I was able to unearth several interesting facts," Tony confirmed as he stirred the cream into the pan and then added the seasonings he'd already pulled from the cabinet.

"Such as?" I asked, hoping that what he'd found was some sort of proof that Star's death was not related to whatever was going on with my father.

"I found out that the man who hired Sam Denton to find proof that your father was still alive is named Layton Henderson."

"And who is Layton Henderson?"

"Mr. Henderson is a billionaire who owns an import-export business that operates around the globe."

Okay, I wasn't expecting that. "And why would a billionaire import-export dealer want proof that my father was alive after all these years?"

Tony began stirring the Parmesan into the milk and butter base. "I'm not sure. I am planning to dig deeper because I suspect there is more going on than is apparent on the surface. It does not make sense that a man with the wealth and resources of this one would care one way or another whether a truck driver from Montana was dead or alive."

"Do you think Henderson had something to do with Star's death? It certainly sounds as if he could afford to have her eliminated if she'd stumbled across information about my father or his interest in him that he didn't want to be made public."

Tony took a whisk to the sauce as the noodles boiled. "I'm honestly not sure. From what I have been able to dig up, Layton Henderson is very well insulated. He lives overseas and rarely comes to the States. We know that your father traveled extensively both before his marriage to your mother and after his fake death, so I suppose it is possible that the two crossed paths. But I'm still not sure that explains why this very powerful billionaire would be looking for your father."

"Yeah, and why hire Denton? He must have his own staff to do that."

Tony picked up the pan with the pasta and drained it into the sink. "I've been thinking about that as well. It did occur to me that Henderson might have found out that Denton was linked to Star, and that Star had been looking for your father. I suppose he might have realized that Denton might already know how to track down the man he was after."

Track down. That made my stomach knot. "Do you think my dad is in danger?"

Tony looked me in the eye. "I don't know."

I took a deep breath as he tossed the pasta with the sauce. I took our wine to the table while he brought the pasta. "So, did you find out anything else?"

Tony took a loaf of French bread from the pantry and sliced it. He carried it to the table as well. "I was able to find out that Star's mother was a twenty-four-year-old woman named Ivana Kowalski."

My eyes grew big. "You know who Star's mother was? That's huge. Do you know why she was with my father and why she was shot and killed?"

Tony shook his head. "I found out her name after managing to dig up the initial police report of the woman who was shot at the time Star was left at the church. I don't know why she was with your father, but I have been able to confirm that the man she was with most likely was your father, as we suspected."

"And anything more?"

Tony twirled the fettuccine with his fork. "I also found a trail of credit card receipts spanning several states and dating back at least several months before Ivana was shot. That indicates to me that she and Grant Tucker were on the move for a while before she died. I don't know why they were running or who shot her, but I'm still looking in to it."

I took a bite of the pasta. It was exccllent, as always. Tony knew just the right spices to use to give his sauces a unique flavor. "This whole thing is a bit overwhelming."

"I know. And I'm sorry. I wish I had the answers you need, but I have a feeling things are going to get a lot more complicated before we get to the bottom of them."

I ate quietly for a few moments. I was having a hard time processing everything. The idea that Star's mother and my father had been friends was hard enough to swallow, but with everything that had happened since, it seemed as if the world as I knew it was once again spinning out of control. Tony had made a good start, but there were still so many unanswered questions. For one thing, we still didn't know what Henderson had done with the photos Denton had taken of my father to prove he was alive, or if the man presented a threat to my father or to anyone else connected to him in the past or the present. Not having all the pieces of the puzzle was frustrating, and nothing Mike and Tony had discovered so far had served as an explanation of why Star had been gunned down in the doorway of her own home.

"Is everything okay?" Tony asked when I'd been quiet for quite some time.

"No. Not in the least. It really does sound as if Star was killed because of her relationship with my father. I'm just not sure how to process that."

"There are circumstances that would point to Star's death and your father's activities as being linked in some way, but we don't know that for certain," Tony reminded me. "I wonder if there was something odd going on with the desk Star bought. Why did she want it so badly? Who did she partner with to get it? Did she ever find the secret compartment? And where is the desk now?"

Tony did have a point. There did seem to be more than one thing involved. "So, what do we do now?" I asked.

Tony hesitated before answering. "In terms of Star's murder specifically, I'm not sure we should do anything at this point. Feathers have been ruffled, so I think it is best we let Mike take the lead. I was asked to look into some very specific things, which I intend to do, but beyond that, I plan to stay firmly on the sidelines and let Mike do his job. Having said that, I am very interested in figuring out why Layton Henderson was interested enough in tracking down your father to hire a PI, and what sort of information Denton provided to him before he died. This may or may not be related to Star's murder, but given the possible threat to your safety as well as Mike's and your mother's, I feel I would be remiss not to do what I can to get some answers."

"You're worried that whoever killed Star might come after us?"

Tony nodded. "I am worried. A lot of people who seem to be connected to your father in one way or another are dead, and I don't know why. Whatever is going on right now seems to me to have originated with Ivana Kowalski's murder, or at least to the series of events leading up to it. I have a list of questions we've asked and asked again but still don't have answers for. Why was she running? Why was your father, who apparently was not the baby's father, with her? Who shot her? Why did your father change his name? Was he working for someone who'd been responsible for protecting her, or was he simply a friend? And why would a billionaire hire a small-town PI to prove a man who had been dead for over a decade was still alive?"

I pushed my plate aside, crossed my arms on the table, and lowered my head. The same questions seemed to be looping back around again and again. I felt like they permeated every thought and every conversation. This really was too much.

Tony got up and walked around the table. I felt him put his hand on my back.

"Having said all that," he spoke softly, "I want you to know I am committed to getting answers to all those questions. And I am committed to making sure you and Mike and your mother are safe while I look for them."

I looked up. "So, are you tracking Dad again?"

"No. I don't want to alert anyone to my search if I can help it. Tracking your dad will put us back on the radar of the same people who threatened us before."

"We need to get the file Star had."

"I agree. And Mike is working on that. In the meantime, I'm going to keep doing what I've been doing."

I looked down at my plate and knew I wouldn't be finishing the food. "Do you want to get back to it now?"

Tony shook his head. "I've been at it all day. I could use a break. I'll do the dishes, and then we'll take the dogs out for a walk. When we get back, I'll check the programs I left running. Hopefully, the pieces of the puzzle we still need will start to fall into place."

"Okay," I agreed. "I'll help you with the dishes."

As it turned out, the walk was an excellent idea. It helped me to both clear my head and relax a bit. I always enjoyed walking along the hard-packed trail Tony maintained for the dogs. Gentle snow added to the ambiance tonight.

When we got back to Tony's place, we fed the animals, and then I followed him down to his computer room so that he could check the progress of his various search engines.

"Did your software find anything?" I asked.

Tony was frowning at the screen but did not answer right away.

"Tony?" I asked again. "Did you find anything?"

He hesitated and then looked toward me. "Actually, I think I have."

I took several steps toward him. I stood behind him, but I couldn't tell what he was looking at. "What did you find?" I asked.

"According to the records I just uncovered, it appears that Ivana Kowalski worked for Layton Henderson for several years prior to becoming pregnant with Star." Tony typed in a few commands that made a series of random codes flash onto the screen.

"That seems relevant. Is that relevant?" I asked.

"It seems as if it might be. If nothing else, it shows a link between Star's mother and Henderson." Tony continued to type commands into the computer. "I don't know specifically when she left the company, but based on these employment records, it appears as if she left her employment with Henderson either shortly before or shortly after becoming pregnant."

My brows flew upward. "Maybe Henderson is Star's biological father," I huffed out.

"Maybe." Tony sounded less than certain as he continued to type. "But that doesn't explain why Ivana ran, why she was with your father, who was chasing them, or who shot her."

I got up and began to pace around the room. Maybe it made more sense than Tony thought. "Ivana was employed by Henderson. Maybe she had a fling with him, and she got pregnant. Maybe Henderson didn't want the baby; maybe he even wanted her to have an abortion. I could see how it might cause a conflict if she refused to do as he asked. He may have felt that if the child was allowed to be born, it would create a liability for him, so he threatened her. Or maybe Ivana didn't want Henderson to know she was pregnant for some reason, and when she found out she was having his child, she left her job and decided to disappear. I suppose she might have been friends with my dad, and he agreed to help her get away from the baby's father."

Tony sat back in his chair. "Okay, say that's true. Say Henderson was Star's biological father and that for whatever reason, Star's mother wanted to put distance between herself and the man who'd fathered her child; that still doesn't explain why Ivana was shot, and it definitely doesn't tell us who shot Star."

I shrugged. "The guy is rich. Very rich. Even if he wasn't a billionaire forty years ago, I would be willing to bet he had substantial assets. Maybe he was afraid that Ivana would make a claim on those assets once she'd delivered his baby, so he decided to get rid of both mom and baby."

Tony narrowed his gaze. "Seems like a stretch."

"Or maybe someone else was afraid that Ivana would make a claim on his assets, so they went after the mother of his unborn child. Was Henderson married at the time of Ivana's pregnancy? Engaged?"

Tony returned his attention to the screen. "I'm not sure. I'll dig around a bit to see what I can find, but keep in mind that at this point, all we know is that Ivana worked for Henderson. The idea that she had an affair with him and that he was the biological father of her child is nothing more than a theory."

"I know, but it is a theory that makes sense to me."

"That's odd," Tony said after he'd been scanning the computer screen for several seconds.

I stopped pacing. "What's odd?"

"According to this, Ivana was transferred from the import-export store in France to a plant in Hungary about eight months before she left Henderson's employ."

"So?"

"So there is no plant in Hungary. At least there isn't one listed in connection with Henderson's import-export business."

"Maybe he operates another type of business in Hungary," I suggested.

Tony frowned. "Maybe. I guess I'll just keep digging to see what else I find."

"Should we tell Mike all this?" I asked.

"I think I should tell him the parts that are fact, such as Star's mother's name and that she worked for Henderson, but I think I should keep the parts that are speculation to us, like our idea that Henderson might be Star's biological father. Mike has a lot on his plate. It doesn't make sense to send him off on a wild-goose chase."

"Agreed. So you'll talk to him?"

"I will. And I'll keep working on this." Tony pulled me into his arms. "Don't worry. We'll figure this out one way or another."

Chapter 6

Friday, December 13

What a week! Not only had the weather been wet and blustery, but Bree and Mike still weren't speaking to me, which made traveling my route stressful. With the Christmas season in full swing, the number of cards and gifts that had been added to my usual delivery schedule made my cold, miserable days even longer than normal. With the short days of winter, it was usually dark when I started my route in the morning and dark again when I finished it. I needed some time to recoup and try to get my bearings, and when I clocked out on Friday, I felt like I'd been granted an eleventh-hour pardon.

"Let's go home," I said to Tilly as I started the Jeep.

Tony and I had discussed where to set up camp for the weekend and had chosen his house, despite the fact that we'd need to drive back into town for the holiday parade and community dinner. We also realized that tomorrow would be a long day, and Tony had a doggy door leading out to an enclosed yard for the dogs, while if we left them at my place, one of us would have to take a break to go let them out halfway through the day.

Tony's house was also a lot larger for the four animals that were going to have to be cooped up all day. It made sense that we stay out at the lake for the weekend.

Besides the animals, Tony had been working with Mike all week and would very likely need access to his computers. My big brother might not be talking to me, but despite the fact that Tony had also kept the secret of Star's birth from him, at least in the beginning, Mike still seemed to think he was the best thing since sliced bread. I'd asked him about it while delivering his mail, and tried to make the point that if he'd forgiven Tony, he should forgive me, and he reminded me that Tony hadn't wanted to lie but had only been doing what I'd asked him to do. Mike was right; I really was the worst. Not only had Tony been doing as I'd asked, but he wasn't Mike's sister and, according to Bree, I'd apparently violated a sibling code.

I had to think about that one for a while, but after I did, I got it. Whatever the truth about our father and his history ended up being, Mike and I should be in this together. He was our father, and we'd both been devastated by his death. I realized that his behavior, good or bad, once revealed, would affect us both equally.

Of course, accepting what I had done and apologizing about a million times hadn't done a thing to repair my relationship with either Mike or Bree, so I decided to set that aside, at least for now, and try to focus on enjoying the weekend. The annual holiday festivities in the small town of White Eagle, Montana, were extensive, and the holiday parade served as the kickoff to the annual fun. In a way, it made no sense to me that the town planned such elaborate outdoor events in December when the weather could range from downright balmy to a total blizzard. But traditions, once established, tended to stick, and someone, at some time, had decided that the town's Christmas celebration would begin with a holiday parade, followed by a spaghetti dinner and a community gathering, and today was the day.

This year, my mother had been enlisted to act as co-chair for the opening day committee, in addition to the Christmas on Main event she'd inherited when the event planner quit. I supposed being asked to serve as chairperson was an honor of sorts, but it was a lot of responsibility, and Mom had been driving me crazy, worrying about everything that could go wrong, from the weather to a pasta shortage, ever since she'd been drafted to organize the dang thing. It had been snowing off and on all week, but the forecast for tomorrow was clear and sunny, which should help alleviate everyone's stress level.

My phone rang as I pulled onto the highway heading up the mountain. I had a hands-free device, so I was able to answer.

"Is everything okay?" Tony asked. "I thought you'd be home by now."

"Yeah. I'm sorry. I should have called to let you know I was running late. I got behind on my route, and then my boss wanted to discuss holiday hours, which begin next week. It was such a long day, and I'm exhausted, but I'm looking forward to the weekend."

"Me too. I have dinner ready. I'll keep it warm."

"I should be there in about fifteen minutes. The roads are icy, so I don't want to push it."

"Take your time. The food will keep. We can even relax with a glass of wine before we eat if you need to decompress."

"That would be nice."

Shortly after I turned onto the lake road, I could see the glow from the hundreds of white lights Tony had strung around his property. Making a mental vow to enjoy the weekend and the season, I took in a deep breath to clear my mind. Although I'd seen Tony every single day this week, I felt like I hadn't spent much time with him. We were both so exhausted by the time the evening came around, we shared mostly silent meals, maybe watched a little TV, then fell into bed with barely a good-night kiss.

Yes, there were good reasons that our lives were so busy and that we'd both become so distracted, but every now and again, we ought to stop to remind ourselves to enjoy the holiday lights.

"I'm home," I called as I walked in the front door.

"I'm in the kitchen. Go ahead and change out of your uniform. I'll grab the wine," he called back.

Sounded good to me, so I greeted Titan, Tang, and Tinder, and then headed up the stairs. God, I was happy to be home. Not only had the tree been lit and the fire started, making the house feel warm and inviting, but whatever Tony was cooking in the kitchen smelled wonderful.

"You look as exhausted as you sounded on the phone," Tony said after kissing me on the lips and handing me a glass of wine as soon as I came down from changing.

"I am as exhausted as I sound, but I'm also very happy to be home and to have two days off, even if one of them is going to be spent helping my mother."

"She called today to remind us not to be late."

I smiled. "I'm sorry. Is she driving you crazy too?"

"Not at all. I love your mom. And I understand why she is frantic. I'm happy to do what I can."

I supposed it was actually kind of sweet that Mom was so comfortable with Tony that she felt she could make him as crazy as she'd been making me.

"So, how was your day?" I asked after we had settled onto the sofa.

"Productive."

"That's good. Do you want to fill me in?"

"Are you sure you want to talk about it right now? We could just relax and let it wait until after we eat."

"I know. And in theory, that does seem like a good idea, but you know me. It is impossible to turn off this brain if there is a question out there waiting to be answered."

Tony nodded. He set his glass on the coffee table in front of us.

"As I've been doing all week, I spent part of my day digging around into the personal and business affairs of Layton Henderson to try to get a better handle on his relationship with Star's mother. I know we speculated that perhaps Henderson was Star's biological father, but somehow that never sat right with me, so I've been actively pursuing alternate theories."

"And?"

"And I found out what Henderson had and continues to have going on in Hungary."

I swiveled just a bit, so I was facing Tony more directly. "And?"

"And I found evidence that Henderson's sideline is really more of a passion. It seems that he is interested in artificial intelligence."

"Artificial intelligence? You mean like robots and stuff?"

"Basically. Initially, Henderson was interested in enhancing and improving the intelligence of his human test subjects by altering elements in their environment. He'd give them specific drug cocktails, or he'd apply a series of rewards and punishments to enhance the learning experience. He was using surgical procedures, restrictive diets, stimulation in vitro. Really anything and everything he could think of to stimulate learning."

"So, he was some sort of Dr. Frankenstein?"

"I don't think he ever built a human out of body parts, but he most definitely tried to control the brain function of those on whom he experimented. At some point, he gave up on trying to improve the human mind and turned his attention to the synthetic one, but forty years ago, he was still trying to figure out how to manipulate people to be their intellectual best."

"Okay, that's creepy. But what does it have to do with Star?"

Tony leaned forward slightly. "What if Ivana was one of Henderson's test subjects?"

"You think that Ivana might have been impregnated as part of some sort of experiment, and when she realized that she was pregnant and that her baby was going to be some sort of lab rat, she ran?"

"I think it is possible. So far, I don't have any evidence to back it up, but I think this is a theory that makes sense."

"So Henderson or his men weren't so much after Ivana as they were after Star, but by the time they caught up with her, Ivana had already given birth, and my father whisked the baby to safety."

"It's a theory."

I did like the fact that in this scenario, my dad was the hero and not the monster. "So if, as the evidence suggests, my father did manage to get away with the baby, and whoever was after Ivana and Star knew my dad was with them, Grant Tucker's life would have been in danger as well. I guess that would explain why he changed his identity and never spoke about his past. But that doesn't tell us who killed Star or why my dad faked his death years after he saved Star."

"I'm still working on who killed Star, but it makes sense that if Star was important to Henderson for some reason, he might not have stopped looking for her, which means he might never have stopped looking for Grant Tucker either. Maybe your dad realized at some point that Henderson was still after him, which is why he faked his death fifteen years ago. Maybe he figured that was the only way to get this very rich and very influential man off his back once and for all."

My hand flew to my mouth. "And then a bunch of years later, we start digging around in Grant

Thomas's death and all but proved he is still alive." This was bad. "If Henderson found out about the photos we'd uncovered, he might have begun his own search by hiring Denton to track Dad down." I gasped. "It is our fault that he is even on Henderson's radar! It is also our fault that he hired a PI, which caused Denton to realize what he had, which got him killed, and most likely got Star killed too."

Tony nodded. "I think so. I know it was never our intention to hurt your father, Denton, Star, or anyone else for that matter, but I'm pretty convinced that all this might have been avoided if we'd never gone looking for your father in the first place."

I closed my eyes and slowly shook my head. "He tried to warn us, but we wouldn't listen."

"I know. I feel horrible about the way things turned out."

I found I had to agree with that, but the theory, as far as theories go, was a lot to swallow. "Even if Henderson did find out that the man who'd hidden the baby he was after was still alive, why did he hire Denton to find him? The man is a billionaire. He must have private security who could have tracked him down."

"The only thing I can come up with is that Henderson knew that Denton was aware of your father after he started looking for Star's birth parents. He might have hoped that Denton would lead him to the baby, who, of course, would be all grown up, living with an unknown name and identity by then, so he hired him to find your father. Maybe Henderson thought that your father had stayed in touch with the baby he'd saved all those years ago."

"But why would Henderson kill Star?"

He shrugged. "I don't know that he did. It really doesn't make much sense that he would."

"Even if Star was conceived as part of some sort of experiment, she seemed perfectly normal," I added. "She didn't seem supersmart, nor did she seem to have superpowers. I can't see how she would be a threat to Henderson or anyone else for that matter, so killing her makes no sense."

"Yet someone did," Tony pointed out.

"And you told all this to Mike?"

"I did. Once I figured out the link between Star and Henderson, I felt that I should."

"I guess Mike knowing is a good thing." I swallowed hard. "Do you think Mom, Mike, and I are in danger?"

Tony paused and then answered. "Mike and I discussed that. I really don't think you are. Grant Tucker did appear to be with Star's mother when she was killed, but that had nothing to do with you or your family. I could be wrong, but I don't think there is a reason for Henderson to want to harm you. And keep in mind, I'm not saying Henderson harmed Star. Again, I can't see why he would have. But there is more of a direct link between Star, her mother, and whatever went on forty years ago, than there is between Henderson and you, Mike, and your mom."

Okay, at least that much was good. Still, if our looking for my dad had resulted in Star's death, I didn't see how I'd ever be able to live with myself.

"How do we prove any of this?" I asked.

"I don't know. As we had all along, it seems that all we really have are a few facts wrapped up in a whole lot of speculation. If the records we need to prove this even exist, it won't be easy to access them."

"Should we even try?"

"Again, I'm not sure. I already feel really responsible, and I wouldn't want our digging around to result in any more deaths."

Tony was right. There was more at stake here than my curiosity about my father's whereabouts since his supposed death. "Do you think my dad was somehow involved with whatever Henderson was doing, assuming, of course, that Henderson really is the bad guy in all this and not just the subject of a story we are telling ourselves, or do you think he was just some guy Ivana knew who agreed to help her?"

He shrugged. "I'm sure I can find additional information if I keep digging. So far, I haven't had the feeling that anyone has even noticed my hacks, but the reality is that it is only a matter of time until someone does. If I continue, I'll be taking a risk, but if I don't, we'll never have our answers."

Tony made a good point. This was definitely complicated. "What does Mike think?"

"He wanted to sleep on it. We're going to talk tomorrow. I think he is curious, as am I, but he also realizes the danger in alerting Henderson that we might know something he doesn't want us to."

"I guess sleeping on it is as good a strategy as any. We could stay up all night going over things again and again, but we need to be alert and energetic for Mom tomorrow, and it won't do us any good to show up exhausted. Besides, if Henderson is behind Star's death, I'm not confident that anyone who digs too deeply won't end up the same way she did."

Chapter 7

Saturday, December 14

I woke up to a bright, sunny sky, which was nice after the series of storms we'd been having all week. Of course, a bright, sunny sky meant that it was later in the morning than I had planned to sleep. Why had Tony let me stay in bed this long? My mom was going to be furious if we were late.

As tempting as it was to lay around in bed all day, I knew I had to get up, so I let my legs slide over the side of the bed. I pulled on a robe and headed toward the kitchen.

"There she is," Tony said to Tilly, who looked relieved to see me.

"What time is it? Why did you let me sleep so long?"

He handed me a cup of coffee. "It's nine o'clock, and we're fine. I fed and walked the dogs, cleaned the cat boxes, and made you a breakfast sandwich you can eat on the way. You showered last night, so all you need to do is pull on some clothes, and we can go." He held up a thermos. "I even have coffee refills for the drive down the mountain."

I couldn't help but smile. It was nice to be pampered. "Thanks for taking care of everything. And it was nice to sleep in, and I do feel better. Just give me fifteen minutes, and I'll be ready."

"I'm going to head out to start the truck so the engine can warm up, but take your time. As long as we leave by nine-thirty, we'll be fine. The parade doesn't start until eleven, so arriving at ten will still be considered early in my book."

"It will. I'll hurry."

Tony put on a station that played Christmas music twenty-four-seven between Thanksgiving and New Year's. It was nice to have that option, but I did wonder if the DJs weren't just a little bit crazy by the time January 1st came around. I mean, there were only so many Christmas songs, and listening to them over and over again must get really old. Of course, I suppose you had the same problem if you worked at a Top 40 station.

"I thought we might walk through the shops in town after the parade, but before the dinner," Tony suggested. "I noticed everyone has their window displays up."

"That sounds like fun, and there will be a break between the two events. I've been wanting to stop by the holiday store."

"Maybe we can get you a tree topper. I noticed you didn't have one. We can get the replacement bulbs we need for the outdoor lights as well."

"The bulbs are fine, but that's a no to the tree topper. It has become the Thomas family tradition not to have one."

Tony raised a brow. "Why?"

"When Mike and I were kids, Mom took charge of making sure the tree got decorated. Mike and I helped, but it was Mom who lugged the decorations down from the attic and strung the lights on the tree. My dad never participated at all until the tree was done, and he'd put the angel on the top. He did it every year. It was his thing. If he wasn't home, we'd wait to add the angel until he got there."

Tony found a parking spot in the lot closest to where the parade would begin. I continued my story as he manipulated his way into the tight space.

"That first year after Dad died, no one wanted to put the angel on the tree. Mike and I thought Mom should do it, and Mom thought one of us should. In the end, no one did, and we didn't have an angel that year. Or the next year, or ever again. If you look closely, you will see that Mom's tree doesn't have a topper either. Mike never really had a tree before Bree, and I'm not sure what she will decide this year, but I continued the Thomas family tradition and skipped the topper once I moved into my own place and began decorating my own tree."

"That's a very touching story," Tony said as he turned off the engine and unbuckled his seat belt. "And one I think we should continue."

"Thank you for understanding."

There were already people mingling around on the street, so after we got out of Tony's truck, we went searching for my mom.

"Oh good, you're here," Mom said when Tony and I found her. "Santa never showed up, and the parade is going to start in less than an hour. Thankfully, Santa is last in the procession, so we have time to get him in the lineup if we can track him down, but we do need to find him, and fast."

"Is Colton Davenport playing Santa again this year?" I asked.

"He is."

Colton Davenport owned a furniture store of sorts. He didn't deal in new furnishings but rather in refurbished items, some valuable and some fairly commonplace. I knew that he lived just outside of town on a small ranch that had space for his workshop. He owned two horses and an antique sleigh he'd refurbished himself and had been acting as Santa for more years than I could remember.

"Colton has been doing this a long time," I reminded my mother. "He knows the drill. I'm sure he'll turn up."

"I hope so, but he has never been this late before. Can you run over to his place to see what's keeping him?"

"Yeah, we can do that," I said to Mom. "I'll call you if there is a problem."

Mom looked toward the street, where those participating in the parade were lining up. "Okay, but hurry. The kids will be so disappointed if there is no Santa to bring up the rear."

Tony and I jumped back into his truck and headed toward Colton's place. I couldn't imagine what was keeping him. I hoped he was okay. Colton was generally the responsible sort, not at all the type to arrive late for his commitments. Tony pulled up outside his house, and I jumped out and headed to the front door. I admired the colorful wreath he'd hung on his door as I knocked and waited for him to answer. When he didn't come to the door after several attempts, I headed toward the old wooden building that served as his barn.

"Colton," I called.

There was no answer. I did see the two horses, which were still in their stalls, and his Santa suit was hanging on a peg on the wall. I knew the sleigh was stored under the large gray tarp in the middle of the barn. It looked like Colton planned to show up for the parade. I really couldn't imagine what had happened.

"He's not here," I said to Tony.

"That's odd. Maybe we should take a look around."

"I tried knocking on the door, and he didn't answer."

"His truck is here," Tony pointed out. "Maybe he is in his workshop, or he was in the shower and didn't hear your knock. Let's take a look in the workshop."

I nodded and followed Tony out of the barn. We headed toward the building that served as his workshop. The door was locked up tight, and a quick peek in the window confirmed that no one was inside. We then headed toward the house and knocked on the front door again. Still no answer.

"Maybe we should look around back," Tony suggested.

"Okay. I'll walk around to the left, and you take the right. We'll meet at the back door."

As I walked around the house, I noticed that one of the upstairs windows was open, which was odd, given how cold it had been, but maybe Colton had found the need to air the place out for some reason. When Tony appeared from around the side of the house, he informed me that he hadn't seen anything that would indicate that anyone was home. I told him about the window. Tony knocked on the back door, calling out all the while. After a moment, I tried the handle. It gave. I glanced at Tony, he shrugged, and we entered the house.

As we walked from the rear of the home toward the front, my heart rate began to increase. Something felt wrong. Very, very wrong.

"Colton?" I gasped when I spotted the man lying on the floor near the front door.

Tony ran over and knelt down. He felt for a pulse and then shook his head.

I pulled out my phone and called Mike. I was surprised by the level of calm I experienced as I informed my brother that there had been another shooting, and he needed to get over to Colton Davenport's place right away. After I hung up, I looked at Tony. "You'll need to be Santa."

"Me?"

"Mom will have a coronary if there is no Santa for the holiday parade. We have the horses and the sleigh. The Santa suit is designed to fit multiple sizes, and Colton was close to your height. Just pull on the pants and jacket over your clothes. I'll call Mom to let her know to stall. If you hurry, you should be able to get there by the time the parade is coming to an end."

"It'll take longer than we have to hook up the sleigh and drive it over there," Tony said.

He did have a point.

"Okay, then just ride one of the horses. This year it will be cowboy Santa who brings up the rear."

Tony hesitated. "Are you sure we shouldn't wait for Mike?"

"I'll wait for him; you go. It doesn't look like anyone was in the barn. I doubt it will be considered part of the crime scene. If Mike balks about the fact that you took the Santa suit and one of the horses, I'll tell him it was my idea. Now hurry. We don't want to let the kids down."

Tony finally did as I asked while I called and briefly filled my mom in. I could tell that she was on the verge of a meltdown. I wasn't sure if that was because Colton was dead, or that she had no Santa. Probably a combination of both. I explained the idea of a cowboy Santa this year, and she actually liked the idea. I promised that Tony would be there as soon as he could, and if she was able to stall, all the better. She assured me that she would tell the school band to take their time, and the floats with the Little League kids and the tikes from the ballet school tended to want to lag once they got started anyway.

Tony pulled on the Santa suit, complete with a fake beard. It would have been great if he'd had a cowboy hat, but because he didn't, we figured the Santa hat that came with the costume would have to do.

"Thanks so much." I quickly kissed Tony through his fluffy, white beard once he was dressed.

"I'm happy to help." We couldn't find a saddle, but we did have reins, so Tony agreed to ride bareback. I hoped he wouldn't fall off, but he seemed comfortable with the situation. He climbed up on a railing and mounted one of the horses, and then Santa took off down the street at a pace that had me clutching my chest.

"Be cool," I said aloud to myself. "Tony knows how to ride. He knows what he's doing. He'll be fine." I took in a deep breath and blew it out. That seemed to help the panic I'd begun to let into my consciousness. I was sure the entire town was going to be devastated when they found out about Colton's death, but I was equally certain that cowboy Santa would be talked about for years to come.

Mike pulled up in his cruiser just as Tony disappeared around a bend. He had the oddest expression on his face as he approached. I decided I wasn't going to bring up our discussion/argument about Dad and Star if he didn't and jumped right in about what Tony and I had found when we arrived at the house.

Mike headed directly toward the body. He pulled on a pair of gloves and checked for a pulse, as Tony had, even though it seemed obvious the guy was dead.

"How long ago did you find the body?" he asked.

"About fifteen minutes ago. I called you immediately upon discovering the body."

Mike's lips tightened. "It took me a little longer to get here than I would have liked because the main road through town is closed due to the parade. Where is Tony?"

"We had the Santa suit that Colton was supposed to wear, so Tony put it on and is covering the parade. We didn't have time to hook up the sleigh, so he is on horseback. Who do you think did this? And why?"

Mike slowly shook his head. "I don't know."

"Do you think that Colton's death and Star's are connected?"

He frowned. "I don't see how they could be, but I also think that it is highly unlikely that a small town like White Eagle would experience two murders in a week without the deaths being related."

I glanced toward the body on the floor. "But as far as I know, Colton had nothing to do with Dad. How could his death be related to Dad and whatever got Star shot?"

"Maybe Star's death had nothing to do with Dad," Mike pointed out. He pulled out a radio and called Frank, who was on his way. He confirmed that the coroner was on his way too and then tossed me a pair of gloves and began to look around. "There doesn't appear to have been any sign of a struggle. I'm going to assume that the killer came to the door and shot Colton as soon as he opened it."

"Just like Star."

Mike nodded. "Yes, just like Star. She fell forward across the threshold, but Colton appears to have fallen backward, away from the doorway. Given the fact that the door was closed, I'm going to assume the shooter closed it. Maybe we'll get lucky and find prints on the doorknob."

"Do you think the guy would be dumb enough to leave prints behind?"

"No. Not really. But it won't hurt to look."

"How long do you think Colton has been lying there?" I asked as I glanced at the body.

"I'm going to guess he was shot sometime this morning, maybe a couple of hours ago. The coroner will be able to provide a better time of death. Tell me again exactly what happened."

I went through everything again, from the time Tony and I had shown up at the parade until Tony had gone off on the horse and Mike had arrived. I had zero ideas why anyone would want to kill Colton. He was a nice man who'd lived in the community for quite some time and was well-liked and respected. He did his part as a volunteer and was a business owner whose store was in good standing with the local merchants association as far as I knew. He was a widower with grown children who lived elsewhere, and a talented artist who could take a dilapidated piece of furniture and make it look new again.

When I'd seen a man get out of a car and gun down Star in cold blood, I had believed her death was directly related to her link with our father. I was less certain of that with Colton. I couldn't imagine any way in which he might be related to Dad, and Mike had made a good point when he'd stated that two shooting deaths in less than a week in our little town almost certainly had to be connected.

Frank showed up while Mike was completing his walk around the house and grounds. I supposed I could take Tony's truck and leave, but Mike hadn't asked me to go, so I chose to stay out of the way but hang around until he kicked me out. My mind was having the hardest time processing everything. If Star hadn't died because of her investigation into her roots, then what on earth was going on?

By the time Mike even remembered I was lurking in the shadows and suggested I go ahead and head back to the parade, it was over. Of course, we still had the spaghetti dinner to get through, but I had time before I was due to show up at the community center to help with the food preparation. I found Tony, still dressed as Santa, holding the reins of his horse and talking to some children when I got back to town.

"The barn manager at the North Pole has been looking for the horse you brought to White Eagle today," I said in an attempt not to spoil the illusion.

"I guess I should get going," Tony replied. He looked at the children. "Remember what I told you about minding your parents."

"We will," they all replied before running toward the group of adults who were standing around waiting for them.

"Let's get the horse back to Colton's place," I said. "I guess you'll have to ride him back. I'll follow in the truck."

Tony agreed to the plan, but first, he stepped into a bathroom to take off his costume. I slipped it into a bag and put that into the truck. I doubted Tony and I would be able to enjoy any part of the relaxing day we'd hoped for, but finding out who had killed Colton was a lot more important. Not that Mike would let me help, but he might let Tony, and that would allow me to be present by association.

When I pulled the truck onto Colton's farm, I could see that Mike was busy with his team, so I gave him his space and just waited inside. Tony arrived a short time later. After he got the horse he'd ridden settled in the barn, he wandered over to speak to Mike. I was tempted to join them but stuck with my decision to wait where I was. Mike had actually been cordial when we'd spoken earlier, which was more than I could say for the way he'd been treating me all week. It seemed like a step in the right direction, and I didn't want to ruin the progress we'd made, so I resisted my natural urge to get involved.

After a while, Tony came over to the truck. "I'm going to stay for a while. I know we talked about going window-shopping, but maybe we can do that later."

"That's fine. I guess I'll head over to the community center to help with the food prep. Maybe Mike can give you a ride over there when you are done here."

He smiled and nodded. "He said he would. And thanks."

"For what?"

"For letting Mike handle this, and for waiting in the wings for your chance to get involved. I think that once Mike thinks about it, he'll realize what a sacrifice you've made. I think it will help."

I tried to prevent the sigh that pushed past my lips. "I hope it helps. I'm ready for us to be friends again." I thought of Bree. "All of us."

When I arrived at the community center, there was a group of women in the kitchen. Unsurprisingly, all conversations revolved around Colton and speculation about the person who'd shot him.

"You know that Colton had been seeing someone from Kalispell," the woman spreading butter on the bread said to the woman in charge of sprinkling on the garlic and Parmesan topping.

"I heard that, but I also heard he broke it off."

"Oh, he did," the first woman agreed. "But it was not an amenable breakup from what I've heard. In fact, I understand that the woman he was seeing has been going around telling anyone who will listen that Colton is a liar and a user. Not that anyone who actually knew him will agree. He was one of the nicest men I've ever met. It just seems that since his wife passed, he has aligned himself with a few women of questionable integrity."

"You aren't trying to say that this woman that Colton had been dating was the one to shoot him?" the woman in charge of dicing the veggies for the salad asked.

"No, of course not," the first woman said. "But when it comes to unrequited love, anything is possible."

Personally, I doubted that Colton had been shot by a spurned lover, but then again, all possibilities would need to be explored. One of the mistakes I'd noticed when viewing the cop shows I liked to watch on TV was that oftentimes the detective in charge of a case settled onto a single suspect or motive too soon and totally missed what was really going on.

"I heard from a few folks I was chatting with after the parade that Colton had gotten himself into a financial bind, and the person he borrowed money from was the sort to break a leg if they weren't repaid," the woman in charge of the sauce joined in.

"Colton isn't having financial problems," the woman dicing veggies countered. "I won't go so far as to say the guy was loaded, but he did okay with his furniture sales. I hear he even went in on a rare desk that was supposedly going to make him and his partner a whole lot of money."

"What kind of desk?" one of the women asked.

"I'm not sure. I just heard a rumor."

"No one is going to shoot a person down in cold blood over a desk," the woman in charge of preparing the pots for the noodles jumped in. "No, if you ask me, Colton most definitely got himself wrapped up with the wrong sort of woman."

Chapter 8

What a long day. It started out horrifically, but by the time the town gathered to share a meal, I'd begun to feel marginally better. After we were done in town, Tony and I headed toward his place on the lake. Tony built a fire while I headed into the kitchen to scrounge around for a snack. The spaghetti dinner in town had been nice, but with so much going on, I hadn't eaten much, and now I was hungry. I made a cheese and fruit plate, added some crackers and a bottle of wine, and took it all into the living room. The dogs were lying on the rug in front of the fire, and the cats, Tang and Tinder, were curled up in one of the big chairs closest to the fire.

I sat down and curled my legs under my body.

"With the exception of discovering that Colton Davenport had been murdered, I'd say the day turned out well," Tony said.

"I guess that is an accurate statement, but wow! I'm still having a hard time with the whole thing.

Colton was such a nice guy. Despite the rumors flying around town, I can't imagine who would kill him in cold blood like that."

"It sounds like there might be something in the information you overheard about the desk it seems that he and Star might have gone in on together."

"I guess. I've been so convinced that my father or someone associated with him killed Star that I never really considered that as an option concerning Star's death. But if the same person did shoot both victims, it seems unlikely that my father is the common denominator." I paused as I watched a burned log roll from the top of the pile. "Did Mike ever get back to you about the preliminary ballistics report from Star's murder? I imagine the first thing we need to determine is whether both Star and Colton were killed by the same gun."

"No. I never did hear what sort of gun killed Star. I can call Mike tomorrow to ask about it."

"If they were killed by the same gun, I think Mike should take a hard look at the estate sale they went to and the items they purchased. They both dealt in old furniture. Star focused on antiques, and Colton bought and refurbished both antiques and common furniture he picked up at garage sales, but they may very well have purchased items from the same sale, and it sounds as if they both extended themselves financially to buy those things."

"It's worth looking in to. Maybe we should start by comparing the phone records of both victims," Tony suggested. "There might be a link that pops out right away. I'll need to use my workhorse in the basement if you'd like to move down there."

"Okay." I picked up the snack I'd just set out and returned it to the kitchen. Tony didn't allow food in the basement, where he kept all his most expensive equipment. He didn't allow animals either, so I made sure the dogs and cats were settled before I followed him downstairs.

There wasn't anything for me to do once I arrived in the cleanroom where Tony worked, so I sat down on a chair near the workstation he chose and watched. Luckily, it didn't take him long to find something to report.

Tony sent several pages of phone records to the large screen on the wall.

"These are the cell phone records for both Star Moonwalker and Colton Davenport. Colton is on the right, and Star is on the left. As it turns out, Colton was using the unlisted number we noticed on Star's phone records when we looked at them earlier in the week."

"So, they were talking to each other?"

Tony nodded and then did a quick count. "They spoke to each other twenty-seven times during the ten days before Star's death."

"Which seems to indicate, as we thought, that they probably were working on something together. Probably something having to do with the estate sale Star participated in. Had the two spoken to each other prior to the rash of calls just before Star's death?" I asked.

"Hang on; I'll check." Tony returned to his computer. It took him several minutes, but eventually, he said, "I found a few random calls between the two over the past six months. No two calls were on the same day or even during the same week, and all of the ones prior to the ten days before Star was murdered lasted less than two minutes."

"So, to me, that sounds as if they knew each other casually, probably as business acquaintances, but something happened a couple of weeks before Star died that launched them into each other's orbit. I'm going to guess that was their partnership on the desk."

"That's the way it looks."

I squinted my eyes and stared at the screen. "Do these records tell you anything else?"

"Not really. I hoped they would have more calls in common, but other than the ones to each other, I'm not seeing many links." Tony paused. "Except this one." He pointed to a number. "This is Celia Bronson's. It looks like she was calling Star on a regular basis, and then she began calling Colton after Star's murder."

"Did you ever speak to her?" I asked.

"I asked her about her calls to Star. She told me that she desperately wanted to buy the desk Star purchased at the estate sale, but Star wouldn't sell. She told me that she called her many times to try to talk her into it. It appears she must have found out that Colton was Star's partner and began working on him to sell her the desk after the shooting. I'll verify that with her tomorrow."

"So if Colton and Star went in on this valuable desk together, where is it?"

"I assume in Colton's possession. Or at least it was before he was shot. I'll ask Mike about it."

Once again, I began to pace. I felt at times that if I wasn't walking, I couldn't think. "You don't think this valuable desk that everyone seems to want is what is really behind both Star and Colton's deaths, do you?"

"I suppose it might be, but it seems unlikely. The desk might be unique and even valuable, but I'm having a hard time believing that anyone would kill two people over a piece of furniture."

"What about the hidden compartment Star was looking for?" I asked. "What if there is something in that compartment that someone either desperately wants or desperately wants not to be found?"

"Like what?"

I shrugged. "In terms of something someone might want, a deed to a piece of land whose ownership is under scrutiny, old bonds that were never cashed, or perhaps a secret recipe that will put a restaurant on the map. In terms of items someone might want not to be found, a diary in which someone confesses to a murder, incriminating photos, a birth certificate that might prove a person is not who they claim to be."

"You read too many novels."

I laughed. "Maybe. But all of that is possible. All of that and a lot more."

Tony nodded. "Okay. I'm sold. It may very well be that it is what is in the desk that someone was willing to kill for, rather than the desk itself."

Chapter 9

Monday, December 16

"Morning, Hap," I called to Hap Hollister, owner of the local home and hardware store, as Tilly and I began our mail route on Monday morning. His store was warm and cozy, and all decked out for the holiday.

"Tess, Tilly. I heard you had some excitement this weekend."

I set a stack of mail on the counter. "Unfortunately, it was not the sort of excitement I welcome. To be honest, my emotions have been all over the map lately. I thought I was okay with everything, but then, about midday yesterday, I realized I wasn't okay at all."

Hap's pale blue eyes crinkled in the corners as he offered me a look of encouragement. "It seems to me that is understandable. Finding the bodies of two people you know within a week of each other seems likely to be the sort of thing that would cause a delayed reaction. Do you have any news about a suspect?"

"No," I said. "Not yet. You know me, though. I'm itching to dig in and get involved, but Tony thinks I should give Mike space to do his job."

"Mike is a good cop." He tilted his head of white hair. "Tony might not be wrong on this one."

I exhaled slowly. "I know. And I know I tend to want to take over, even though solving crimes is not my job. But I find it hard to sit on the sidelines. I have to admit it took all my willpower not to start my route at Mike's office this morning so I could casually ask how things were going, but it will seem less suspicious if I do my route in the usual order." I took a piece of hard candy from Hap's jar. "I don't suppose you've heard anything?"

"Probably nothing that you don't already know. Folks are slim on facts, but there has been a lot of speculation."

"What sort of speculation?" I asked.

"A few folks figure that Star and Colton had a thing going on. A romantic thing," Hap emphasized. "And then there are a few folks who figure that there must be an ex involved who wasn't happy about them hooking up."

I raised a brow as I slipped my bag off my shoulder and set it on the floor next to Tilly. "A thing? Do you know for a fact that they were seeing each other?"

He shook his head. "I don't know it for a fact myself. I guess the two had been seen together a couple of times in the past few weeks. You know how rumors get started. You share a meal, and the next thing you know, everyone is saying you are having a thing."

Chances were, they were just discussing their business deal, but I didn't say as much to Hap because I wasn't sure what was public knowledge and what was not. "It might have just been a meal between friends," I finally said.

"I don't know. They were seen sharing a platter of wings and a pitcher of beer. Seems like a date to me."

"Did they look intimate?" I asked.

Hap shrugged. "How would I know? They were seen eating and talking. It's not like they were going at it right there in the bar. Still, I heard there was a vibe if you know what I mean."

I supposed it was possible the pair were both dating and business partners. In fact, it seemed entirely possible that one thing led to the other. "Any other theories?"

"Lots of talk going around, but nothing I would bank on. I'd be willing to bet that with your cop brother and genius boyfriend, if anyone knows the real scoop, it is probably you."

I slipped my bag back onto my shoulder. "Normally, that would be true, but Tony and I agreed to stay out of Mike's way. If you hear anything, text me. You have my number."

After I left, I found myself wondering what sort of conclusions investigators might come to if they pulled my phone records with the intent of analyzing them. I was something of a busybody, and I did tend to talk to a lot of random people about a lot of different things every day. Still, there probably weren't any red flags in my phone records. At least I didn't think there were unless you added in the fact that the location of cell phone calls could be estimated, and I'd spent a lot of time talking to Tony while I sat in front of Star's house. If I were a suspect in her murder, the fact that I'd spent so much time watching her would definitely come into play.

I felt my anxiety rise as I neared Mike's office. I'd intentionally made myself wait until as close to the time of my usual mail drop-off time as possible, but the longer I waited, the more nervous I became. I hoped that our interaction at Colton's place on Saturday had served as an icebreaker that would allow us to repair our relationship. Of course, there was no way to know if his willingness to speak to me then would extend into our day-to-day lives. I wouldn't know that until I tested the water.

By the time I arrived at the police station, my palms were sweaty despite the cold, but I took a deep breath and forged ahead.

"Tess, Tilly," Frank greeted us with genuine enthusiasm.

"Hey, Frank," I returned while at the same time bracing myself as the sound of a hundred-pound dog running at full speed came from the hallway. "And hello, Leonard," I said to Mike's dog, who jumped up to say hi. He licked me across the face, and then trotted over to say hi to Tilly. "It looks like you got cards today." I set the pile of mail on Frank's desk.

"I decided to start a board because your mom and aunt have had so much fun with their cards-from-across-the-world thing."

Mom and Ruthie had begun asking the customers who stopped in throughout the year to send them

Christmas cards for their wall, and the effort had grown to include some from around the globe.

"Your board looks nice," I said.

"I'm just getting started, but so far, I've gotten cards from twenty states. By the way, Mike wanted me to ask you to pop your head in his office while you were here if you had a minute."

Okay, Tess, stay cool, I reminded myself. "Yeah, I have a few minutes. I'll just leave Tilly here to visit with you and Leonard."

Prior to the disagreement with Mike that had affected our relationship so much, we'd actually gotten along really well. I was determined to do whatever I could to fix things, no matter how hard it might be to remain in the shadows.

"Hey, Mike," I greeted him. "Frank said you needed to talk to me."

"Yeah. Come on in and have a seat."

I did as he indicated.

"I spoke to Tony this morning," he continued. "He had some interesting things to say about the phone records of Star and Colton, and it got me to thinking about the fact that you had been stalking Star for weeks before her death."

"Following her," I corrected him.

"Whatever. The point is that you were watching her. Maybe you saw something."

I furrowed my brow. "Like what?"

Mike tapped the end of his pen rhythmically on the desk. "Maybe you noticed someone Star spoke to or somewhere she went. Maybe you overheard a conversation while you were in her shop. I'm not sure what I am looking for exactly, but it sounds like you were paying as much attention to her comings and goings as anyone during her last weeks on earth."

He had a point. I had been following her for quite a while by the time she died. Even longer than Mike seemed to realize. Maybe I did know something. I tried to think back.

"There were people in and out of her shop while I was there," I started. "Some I knew, most I didn't. I don't remember anyone acting odd, and I don't remember anyone being around more than once while I was there." I bit my lower lip as I processed the information I'd stored away. "There was this one lady who was looking for a specific sort of desk. I know that Star spoke to her on several occasions because she mentioned previous conversations. But I didn't notice any tension between the two of them, or anything that would explain Star being shot down in her doorway. I have heard that Star purchased an expensive desk shortly before her death, but I'm not sure that the woman I saw in Star's store was looking for that particular desk. I imagine she sold a lot of desks."

"What about people coming and going from her house or strange cars parked in front?"

I paused and thought about it. "Star went out from time to time. I'd see her arrive at home and then leave again a short time later. I never followed her, though."

"I guess that's something."

I wanted to remind Mike that I was simply trying to protect the woman, but even I was no longer sure that was the real motive behind my actions.

"There was a neighbor who lived behind Star. Short woman. Short blond hair. Looked to be in her sixties, if I had to guess. I'd see her walk around the corner and stop in and say hi to Star from time to time. They seemed to be friends of sorts. I don't know her name, but I suppose it would be easy to find that out. It seems to me that she was around often enough that if something significant was going on in Star's life, they might have discussed it."

"Anyone else?" Mike asked.

"No. I don't think so. Hap mentioned that he heard that Star and Colton were together a while back. They were in the bar, sharing a pitcher of beer and a plate of chicken wings."

Mike tossed his pen onto the desk. "I heard that, as well. It looks like they did partner on the desk Star had been trying to get a loan to buy. Star and Colton most likely met to talk about that."

"Maybe. But Hap said there was a rumor going around that their meeting had a vibe that felt more date-like."

"When did Hap tell you that?"

"Just a little while ago. When I stopped in to deliver his mail. He said that folks are talking, which I suppose is natural given the situation. Still, you might want to stop by to chat with him."

"I will. Anything else?"

I slowly moved my head from left to right. "Not that I can think of. I can call you if I do think of anything. If you want me to, that is."

Mike nodded. "I do want you to call if you think of anything. I'm still not sure how this is all going to play out, but it does look as if Star and Colton were shot by the same person. The bullet size and type match. I'm waiting for a detailed ballistics report to confirm whether the same gun was used."

"So Star's death most likely had nothing to do with our dad or her past?"

Mike shook his head. "Probably not."

"I guess I'm glad to hear that, but I'm also surprised."

Mike blew out a breath. I noticed for the first time how tired he looked. "Yeah, me too. Tony is working on some stuff for me. At this point, I'm just hoping that something he finds helps us to make sense of things because right now, I'm lost."

"You'll figure it out; you always do." I stood up. "Call me if you need me."

With that, I left. I wanted to say more. I wanted to launch into a whole new round of apologies, but I figured the door had been opened a crack, and it seemed like a good idea to get out of there before I said something that would cause it to slam closed again.

Chapter 10

By the time I'd made it to Sisters' Diner, they'd closed for the day, so the only people inside the restaurant, other than Mom and Ruthie were the busboy and the soda delivery guy.

"Your wall looks really nice." I paused to admire the cards, which already covered most of the wall. Mom and Ruthie had been doing the wall for three years, and in that time, they had gained quite a following. "I have more cards today." I held up the stack of mail.

"Oh good," Ruthie said. "We have this one bare spot that has been bothering me all day."

I turned to Mom. "So, how are you doing now that the parade is behind you?"

"I felt better for about two minutes, and then I remembered that it is only five days until Christmas on Main, and I began to panic again."

"How did you end up as chairperson for both the parade and Christmas on Main?" asked the busboy.

Mom let out a sigh. "I don't know. I really don't. I specifically remember that I was the one who stood up at the meeting we had way back in the fall and said that adding the traveling carnival to Christmas on Main would be just too much. I have no idea how I ended up letting the others talk me into hiring the event planner, and I really don't have a clue how the group manipulated me into overseeing the aforementioned woman. Never again, I tell you. Never again."

"It'll be fine," I said in my most comforting voice. "The carnival will begin Friday evening, and then the main craft portion of the event will run alongside the carnival on Saturday and Sunday, and by Monday, you will be all done."

"Sounds easy when you say it, but you aren't the one who is short two food vendors and several volunteers to run the ticket booth."

"I can't cook, but I can help with the tickets," I offered. "And Bree can cook. I'm sure if you ask her, she'll help as well. And you can always count on Tony to cook or sell tickets or handle pretty much anything."

"I know. And I appreciate that."

"If you ask me, all this planning is a waste of time," the man refilling the soda machine said.

"And why is that?" I asked.

"You did hear about the big storm that is supposed to come through this weekend, didn't you?"

"Storm?" Mom screeched. "Did you say storm?"

"I hear it's going to be a full-on blizzard," the man confirmed.

"But it has been so nice," Ruthie said.

The man shrugged. "You know what they say about the calm before the storm?" He wiped his hands and then passed a clipboard to Ruthie. "If you'll just sign here, I'll be on my way."

I pulled out my phone and pulled up my weather app. Egad—it was supposed to snow this weekend. And not fluffy snow for effect, but a full-on blizzard, just as the man had said. There was no way the carnival would be able to operate in a snowstorm. In fact, there was no way anyone would be out and about if it did wind up snowing as hard as the app indicated.

I glanced at Mom, who looked white as a sheet.

"What are we going to do?" she asked, panic evident in her voice.

"I'm sure the committee has a plan in place in case of snow," I said.

"Sure. We did. Last year, when the event consisted of some craft booths and a few food vendors," Mom answered. "The old plan was to move everything inside to the community center, but I don't think the tilt-a-whirl or merry-go-round are going to fit in the community center. Why on earth did we let that woman talk us into something that was so much larger than we could manage?"

What I really wanted to ask was why on earth the committee would sign a contract with an out clause for the coordinator, but I decided to hold my tongue. I was just getting Mike to talk to me again; I didn't want to make my mother mad at me as well.

"Maybe it's not too late to cancel the carnival," I said. "You could put a notice in the newspaper and maybe post flyers around town to let folks know the event will consist of those activities that can be held indoors."

"If we cancel the carnival, we still have to pay the company the minimum we promised them. It's in the contract."

"Okay, then maybe you should just proceed as planned and hope the storm veers to the north or the south or anywhere other than here," I suggested.

"Storms peter out all the time," Ruthie added.

"That's true," Mom said. "And the weather app is only right about half the time. I'm sure things will be fine."

I could tell by the tone of her voice that she didn't believe that, but I had to hand it to her for at least trying to keep it together.

Sisters' Diner was my last stop of the day, so after I did what I could to comfort Mom, I headed home. I loved the fact that Tony was waiting there for me. The thought of him busy in the kitchen brought a smile to my face even on a difficult day. Of course, he wasn't always there waiting for me. His job took him away for long periods of time. In the beginning, I hadn't minded it, but now that we were basically living together, I found it harder and harder to say goodbye.

"What smells so good?" I asked as I walked in through the front door.

"Lasagna. It'll be about thirty more minutes. Do you want a glass of wine?"

"Yes, please. I'm going to change first." I greeted Titan, Tang, and Tinder, and then headed toward my bedroom.

"You fixed the lights on the tree," I called back as I noticed that the lights that had been flickering last night shone bright and steady this evening.

"I just replaced the string."

I accepted the wine from Tony as I emerged from the bedroom.

"So, how was your day?" he asked.

"Okay. When I dropped off the mail at the police station, Mike actually talked to me. I consider that progress."

"I agree. That *is* progress."

"He mentioned that the two of you had talked, and he asked me what I might have observed while I was following Star around."

"Did you remember anything?" Tony asked.

"Not really. Did you make any headway today?"

Tony shook his head. "I did some research on the desk that Star and Colton purchased. I was able to confirm the year it was made, as well as the name of the artist who made it. It does look as if he was known for adding hidden drawers or compartments in his pieces. I've been thinking about our conversation about the possible contents of the desk, and the more I think about it, the more convinced I am that you might have been on to something when you suggested that the contents of the desk could be the motive for the killings."

"So we just need to find the desk and then find the hidden drawer and open it. If we do all that, we could have our motive for murder."

"If we are correct in our assumptions and if whatever was in the desk is still there."

"You think that Star and Colton might have figured out the hiding place and taken out whatever was inside?"

"I think that is a possibility."

"Okay, so if there was something in the desk that someone wanted badly enough to kill for it was moved, where would it be now?"

Tony lifted a shoulder. "Maybe in either Star or Colton's home? Or perhaps one of their places of business?"

"Star died a week before Colton. If she had whatever it is that someone is after, it seems like Colton would have gone to get it. I think we should call Mike to suggest that we go out to Colton's to take another look around."

After a discussion between Mike and Tony, it was decided that we'd all take a second look together. Tony turned off the oven and left the lasagna to cool. We'd either eat it when we got home or reheat it tomorrow.

When we arrived at Colton's house, I realized that not only was Mike waiting for us but Bree as well. I greeted her warmly, but her greeting in response was barely more than a grunt. Yep, this was going to take some time.

Mike handed pairs of gloves to each of us. He suggested that we break up, and each pair take a floor of Colton's two-story house. The plan was to search the house for the desk or any documents that looked old or important, then the workshop, and then Star's house, and finally, both Star's antique shop and Colton's furniture store.

Mike and Bree took the first floor, and Tony and I went up to the second floor. Colton's home office was on the first floor, which seemed to me to be the best location to find documents if there were any, but his bedroom was upstairs, which I supposed was equally as likely a place for Colton to stash documents, perhaps in his closet.

"I wonder if either Star or Colton had a safe," I mused to Tony as he dug through the closet, while I searched through the nightstand and dresser.

"I suppose they might have. It seems like a safe would be built into the wall or the floor of either the office or the bedroom. I'll look for something in here."

I dumped the contents of the nightstand onto the bed. A flashlight, a half-read novel, a pad and pencil, hand lotion, lip balm, and a pair of glasses. I carefully ran my hand around the drawer of the nightstand in search of a hidden bottom, but there didn't appear to be one, so I began putting everything away. Before I returned the notepad, I noticed that the first page had something written on it.

"'LD1492 – SM1019,'" I said aloud. I had no idea what it meant, but I tore off the sheet of paper and put it in my pocket.

I headed toward the dresser and found the clothing I expected, along with an envelope containing miscellaneous receipts. You'd think Colton would keep his receipts in his office, but maybe he liked to balance his checkbook while sitting in bed.

"Did you find anything?" I asked Tony when he emerged from the closet.

"Just this file box with old customer records. I thumbed through and didn't find anything current or anything that looked like it was worth killing for. How about you?"

I handed Tony the numbers and letters I found on the first sheet of the notepad. "What do you make of this?"

"I have no idea. Let's show it to Mike. We'll take a look in the bathroom and guest room and then head downstairs."

The guest room contained a bed, a television, and a small dresser but was otherwise empty. The bathroom had all the usual things you'd find in a bathroom, plus a prescription for blood pressure medication and antifungal cream. Nothing that would explain why someone would shoot the guy. Tony and I headed down to join Mike and Bree. Maybe they'd had more luck in the office.

"Find anything?" I asked when we found them in the office.

"Not much. Bree found a pad with handwritten notes on it in the kitchen near the phone. They don't appear to have anything to do with the desk or something that might have been found in it, but I am going to take it with us anyway. How about you guys?"

I handed Mike the page I'd torn from the pad by the bed. "I have no idea what this means, but it could be something. You didn't find a safe?"

"No. It doesn't appear that Colton had one, although he must have had one somewhere. I doubt he kept his cash receipts just lying around, and I doubt he went to the bank every day. It's possible he might have, but he didn't seem to do the volume of business that would require it."

"I imagine he might have a safe in the office at the furniture store," Tony responded.

"That was my thought as well," Mike agreed. "I don't think there are any documents here in the house. Bree and I will check out the workshop, and you and Tess can look around in the barn."

I didn't think we'd find anything in the barn, but following Mike's dictates seemed like a good idea, so I nodded, took Tony's hand, and headed in that direction.

"I wonder what happened to the horses," I said when we entered the barn and found it empty.

"Someone must have come by to pick them up. Perhaps a neighbor."

"I guess that makes sense. They'd need to be cared for." I stood in the middle of the barn and looked around. "Do you think there could be anything to find in here? This isn't even a secure building. I don't see Colton stashing anything of value in here."

"I agreed it is unlikely that we will find anything, but Mike asked us to take a look, so we'll take a look. There is that little storage room in the back. Let's start there."

We looked through the storage room, looked in each stall, checked all the walls, and even stomped around on the floor, looking for a hidden space beneath it. We were about to leave when something told me to pull up the tarp covering the sleigh. "Well, would you look at that?" I pulled away the rest of the tarp to reveal a large desk sitting next to the sleigh. I slid one of the drawers open. As expected, it was empty.

"If there were ever any documents in this desk worth killing for, I doubt they are still there," Tony said. "Let's tell Mike what we found and see what he wants to do."

Mike and Tony loaded the desk into his truck and then transported it down to the police station. Mike felt the desk should be locked up in the evidence room until he could decide what should be done with it. Once it was covered and secured, we headed to Star's home and then we headed into town to take a looked around Colton's furniture store and Star's antique store. We didn't find any documents, but visiting Star's home and store did make me wonder what would happen to all her stuff. Her adoptive parents were dead, and she didn't have any siblings. She'd also never married nor had children. I supposed next of kin was something the courts would need to figure out, but it made me sad that at the time of her death, she was seemingly alone in the world.

Chapter 11

Thursday, December 19

With Christmas at Main starting the next day, local gossip had segued from the shooting deaths of Star and Colton to the carnival that had rolled into town and begun to set up. So far, the storm that was threating to ruin everyone's fun had remained to the south of us, but I knew how unpredictable storms could be. If the storm did remain to the south, I was sure the locals would get a kick out of the merry-go-round, tilt-a-whirl, and Ferris wheel. But if the storm veered north from its current course even a tiny bit, there was no way any of those rides could run.

I really hoped for Mom's sake that things went off without a hitch. There had been enough stress in the Thomas family this week already. Mike still hadn't found the documents we suspected had been hidden in the secret compartment of the desk, nor had he been able to narrow down who might have shot and killed these popular White Eagle residents. Of course, there might never have been any documents inside the desk, and even if there had been, we were just assuming that Star and Colton had been able to open the secret compartment to retrieve them. I supposed if there had been any documents, they were still as hidden as they'd always been, although it was Austin Wade's opinion that if they hadn't found and opened the secret drawer, Star would have kept calling him, and after the last set of hints he'd provided, the calls had stopped altogether, which, in his mind, indicated that she'd been successful.

Tony was still helping Mike, as was I, to the extent he allowed me to do so. It did seem as if Mike's mood toward me had softened, and he'd actually greeted me with a smile and enthusiasm in his voice when I'd dropped off his mail yesterday. Bree was still acting as icily as ever. I'd tried to give her time, but I knew that if she was going to forgive me for lying to her husband, it was going to take more than time.

"Morning, Hattie," I greeted her as I walked in through the front door of her bakeshop. "Something smells good."

"I'm baking the gingerbread men I signed up to sell at Christmas on Main this morning. I'm afraid I got a late start, but this is the last batch."

"Late start? The event doesn't even begin until tomorrow evening."

"True, but the baking is the easy part. Once they are made, I still have to decorate several hundred cookies."

I could see how that would be time-consuming. Hattie explained that each cookie would be decorated to be somewhat different from all the others. Not that there were several hundred combinations, but some were smiling, some frowning, and others were given an "O" of surprise where the mouth ought to be. In addition, some had hats, others jackets, a few boots, and there were even some with overalls.

"I don't suppose you would sell me one early," I said.

"I have some broken pieces you can have if you're just hungry."

"No, it's not that. What I really need is an 'I'm sorry' cookie to bring to Bree."

"Ah." She nodded. "I heard the two of you had a spat."

"I think this has been more than a spat. I've apologized a bunch of times, but I think I need to make a grand gesture."

"Come on back in an hour. I'll have something special for you to give to Bree."

I reached forward and hugged Hattie. "Thank you so much. This means a lot."

"Seems like it has been a tough week for the whole Thomas family. How is Mike doing with his investigation?"

"He's pretty much got nothing. Well, maybe not nothing. I know he has some leads he is tracking down, and Tony is following up on some things for him, but so far, every lead has led to a dead end. Still, I'm sure he'll figure it out given enough time. With the two deaths being treated as a single event in terms of killer and motive, it narrows things down, but maybe too much. If things don't start to come together soon, I think he may need to widen the search parameters."

"Mike will figure it out. Sometimes these things take time."

"I guess that's true."

"So, how is your mom holding up?" Hattie asked.

"She is pretty stressed. I'm helping her as much as I can, but I've been busy, and the event planner left her with a huge mess. Not only does she have the regular Christmas on Main events to keep track of, but with the added carnival and the impending storm, I'm afraid she is about to go over the edge."

"Sounds like she might need a cookie as well."

I smiled. "Actually, if you have time, that would be great. Sometimes a small gesture that lets you know that you're not alone really helps."

I promised to be back in an hour, and Tilly and I continued on our way. It was overcast but dry, and the wind had yet to kick up, so maybe the storm would miss us, as we hoped. I decided to alter my route a bit to catch Mom, Mike, and Bree after I picked up the treats from Hattie. I still needed to go by to drop off the mail for Sue Wade, Austin's niece and the owner of the local sewing store, so I headed there next. Her shop wasn't far from Colton's furniture store, and although I had no mail to deliver to the now permanently closed business, I decided to take a detour and walk past the shop anyway.

It made me feel sad that the business that Colton had poured so much of his energy into could simply go away. Unlike Star, Colton did have children, although they lived out of the area, and I assumed that at some point, they'd come around to clear out his possessions.

As I stood looking in through the front window, I noticed that something seemed different than it had when Mike, Bree, Tony, and I had been here on Monday evening. At first, I couldn't put my finger on it, but then I realized that the large painting of the town back in the fifties, which Colton had hung on the back wall, had been taken down and set on the floor. I supposed Mike might have moved it for some reason, but in the event he hadn't, I figured I should call him about it.

"Hey, Mike," I said after calling his cell. "I was passing by Colton's furniture store on my way to deliver Sue's mail when I noticed that large painting Colton had hanging on the back wall is now on the floor. I wanted to make sure you moved it, and that the place hadn't been broken in to."

"You were passing by Colton's place on the way to drop off mail for Sue?"

I should have known that Mike would realize that I actually would have had to walk a block out of the way to pass by Colton's store, but I didn't think that was the point. "So, did you move the painting?" I asked, deciding to avoid his question.

"No, I didn't move it. Are you there now?"

"I am."

"Okay. I'll be there in a few minutes."

Mike had a key to the store, so he let us in when he arrived. It became obvious as we walked around that someone had been inside and had moved things around. It also seemed as if they had tried to put things back. Chances were they'd managed to lift the large painting down off the wall but then found it too heavy to lift back up and so had left it leaning against a wall. They'd done a good enough job replacing the other furniture that they'd moved; I probably wouldn't have noticed it if not for the painting.

"Someone has definitely been in here. I'm going to have Frank come by to take some prints." Mike had brought gloves for both of us, and I'd had Tilly wait by the front door so as not to contaminate things. "Can you tell if anything is missing?"

I looked around. "I'm not sure. It's not like I memorized the inventory when we were here. I realized that the painting had been moved; otherwise, I wouldn't have noticed the rest. But there are scrape marks on the floor that disturbed the dust, so it does seem that someone was in here looking around. I sure don't remember any of us moving the furniture when we were here on Monday."

"No. We were careful. It does look like someone has been inside the store since then. Good job noticing the painting. Maybe if we can find a print, we can figure out who was here."

I smiled when Mike complimented me but didn't make a big deal about it. I simply told him that I was happy to help and was going to continue on my way, and if he had any more questions for me, I'd be by his office in a couple of hours with the mail. With that, I continued on toward Sue's Sewing Nook.

Sue had lived in White Eagle her entire life, and she was a Wade, so folks tended to talk to her. Maybe she had some insight into the events of the past couple of weeks.

"Tess, Tilly," Sue greeted us. "It's so nice to see you. It's been a few weeks."

"You haven't had mail for a few weeks." I set an envelope on her counter. "I think even this may just be an ad, but it is my job to deliver it, so here it is."

She picked it up, looked at it, and tossed it in the trash. "It is true that I have most of my mail sent to the house, but every now and then something shows up here. I hear that you were the one who found poor Colton's body."

I nodded. "Yes. I went by to check on him because he was late for the parade and found him lying on the floor of his house."

"I did see Tony riding through town in the Santa suit. It was nice of him to cover, but I was devastated when I found out why Colton hadn't made it. And to find out that he'd been murdered so soon after Star Moonwalker. What is this world coming to?"

I slipped my bag off my shoulder and set it on the floor. "I don't suppose you might have heard who was responsible for the deaths?"

"Well, there has been talk. You know how it is in a small town. But I don't think anyone knows for certain. Before Colton's death, there were a few people who thought the man who showed up in Star's shop a few days before her death might have been responsible, but after Colton was shot too, I think the popular opinion is that one person is responsible for both deaths."

I narrowed my gaze. "What man? You said a man showed up at Star's shop. What was his name, and why did people think he killed Star?"

"I don't know his name offhand. Jillian, from over at the pharmacy, was the one to tell me about it, so she might know. She said that the guy looked like he was from the government. He wore a black suit and had a listening device in his ear, so he definitely wasn't from around here."

"Could the listening device have been a Bluetooth device for a cell phone?"

"I guess it might have been. Jillian just said that the man looked like a fed, maybe CIA. He had this real commanding presence, and he never smiled once while she was there."

"Did she know why the man was there?"

Sue shook her head. "She said he came in and asked Star if she was Star Moonwalker. She said she was, and then he said he had some questions for her, and he kicked Jillian out, locked the door, and turned the 'open' sign to 'closed.'"

"He kicked her out?"

She nodded. "Jillian was the only customer at the time. She'd been getting ready to check out when the guy showed up, but before she could even set her stuff on the counter, the guy announced that the store was closed, and that was that. If you want to hear more about it, you can talk to Jillian directly."

"I will. And thank you. I appreciate the information."

"I just want the killer found. Two locals killed in just over a week has everyone on edge. What if this guy is some sort of a serial killer who isn't done doing whatever it is he feels he needs to do? Who might be next?"

It had never occurred to me that the person who had shot Star and Colton was a serial killer on a spree, but I guess I could see how others might be concerned about that very thing.

"I know that you like to collect antiques."

"Yes. Good quality antiques are one of my vices, I'm afraid," Sue confirmed.

"Had you heard that Colton and Star had gone in together to buy a desk from the Colonial era?"

"I had heard. I spoke to Uncle Austin about it. He seemed to think the desk might have a hidden drawer, but I think it is more likely the one they had was the kind with a false back."

"Do you have any idea how to get to the false back?"

She shrugged. "I have a few. If the desk is the type I am thinking of, there will be a small knob in the back of the center drawer. It won't seem like much, and you really need to feel around to find it, but if you do, and you turn the knob all the way to the left as far as it can go and then give the knob a little tug, a sort of latch should appear. All you need to do once you find that latch is give it a pull and the panel will pop open."

I figured it couldn't hurt to try what Sue suggested, so I called Mike to tell him what I'd learned. He was still at the furniture store, so he arranged to meet me at his office at around five.

Chapter 12

Jillian Brown had worked at the local pharmacy for three or four years, a woman I guessed to be in her late forties. Her children were all married or in college, which left the big old house she'd raised them in in Missoula feel much too large and much too empty, she said, so she sold it and moved to White Eagle. Jillian was a nice woman who I didn't know super well, but we had spoken on occasion. She could be found at the pharmacy Monday through Friday from nine to five, and at the local flea market, selling her artwork, on the weekends. At least during the summer. The flea market was closed between November 1 and April 1, but there were often local events, such as this weekend's Christmas on Main, where local artists could peddle their work.

"Afternoon, Jillian," I greeted her as Tilly and I wandered in from the street.

"Hey, Tess. What are you doing here? The pharmacy has a box down at the post office."

"I'm not here with mail. I'm actually here to ask you about the man you saw at Star's store right before she died. The one who kicked you out."

Her lips tightened. "The guy was totally rude. It was late, near closing time, but Star always lets me finish shopping rather than kicking me out if I get there before she actually locks the door. This man pulled up in a dark sedan—black, I think, but I can't be sure. I do remember it had dark, tinted windows. After he parked, he came in and started acting like he owned the place. He asked Star if she was indeed Star Moonwalker, and when she said she was, he announced that the store was closed and that I'd need to leave. I hadn't even had a chance to pay for the items I'd picked out. The guy was a real buffoon."

"Did he happen to identify himself?"

"No. He never said who he was. That's weird, right? Aren't people who work for the government supposed to show a badge and state their name right off the bat?"

"They are. And yes, it was odd if this man did work for the government that he didn't identify himself. Do you have reason to believe he worked for the government?"

"He just had that look about him, if you know what I mean."

I did know what she meant. "Did Star ever tell you who the man was or what he wanted?"

"No. I went by her place the next day to ask her about it, and she told me that he had some questions for her that she couldn't discuss. She told me that everything was fine and that I shouldn't worry about it, but she had this look in her eye that told me there was more going on than she wanted to say. I tried to get more out of her, but she said she needed to make a phone call, and then she offered me a twenty percent discount on everything I'd picked out the previous day, plus anything I wanted to add to the pile right then. I guess I became somewhat distracted at that point; I went just a bit crazy with the twenty percent discount."

"And she never brought it up again after that?"

"I never saw her again. After she checked me out and gave me my discount, I left. I stopped by the next day, but there was a sign in her window saying that she'd be closed for a few days. The next thing I knew, she was dead."

"And what day did you see the sign saying she was going to be closed?"

Jillian paused to think about it. "I guess it must have been a Friday."

Star died on a Friday. I wondered if Mike knew she'd closed her shop that day.

"Can you describe the man you saw?" I asked.

"Tall. Dark hair. Thin. He had dark eyes and dominant cheekbones. Bushy brows and thick lips. Oh, and he had something in his ear. A listening device, I think."

I supposed the man Jillian described could be the same one I'd seen shoot Star. That guy was tall and thin with dark hair, but I hadn't seen his face, and he was wearing casual clothing rather than a suit. I was pretty sure his car had been dark blue rather than black, but it was dark, so I supposed I might have been wrong, or perhaps Jillian was the one who was wrong about the color of the car she'd seen. I sincerely doubted this guy was a fed, or he would have shown his badge and given his name. But if he wasn't FBI or CIA, who was he and what had he come to the shop to discuss with Star? More importantly, had their discussion gotten her killed?

I thanked Jillian and continued on. It was time to stop by to pick up my treats from Hattie, so I headed in that direction. If the man Jillian had seen in Star's place was the one who killed her, could he have been the same one who killed Colton? They had been partnering on a project, so it seemed to make sense that they'd both died as a result of something having to do with it, but was that the only explanation? I knew it couldn't be.

I picked up my box of sweets from Hattie and went to the diner first because I knew my mom would be happy to see me. She was busy because the restaurant was still open, but I gave her the good-luck treat and reminded her that she wasn't in this alone. She thanked me and told me that it helped to know she had me in her corner. Again, after all the people who'd been mad at me this week, I was happy to talk to someone who wasn't.

After I left Sisters' Diner, I went straight to the Book Boutique. Bree had been abrupt but polite when I'd delivered her mail this week. I just hoped the apology pie that Hattie had made for me would do the trick.

"Afternoon, Bree," I said cheerily as I laid her stack of mail on the counter.

"I don't have outgoing today."

I slipped my bag onto the floor while Tilly trotted around the counter to say hi to Bree. My best friend and sister-in-law might be mad at me, but she wasn't mad at Tilly and had a dog cookie waiting for her.

"I brought you something," I said.

That seemed to get her attention.

"It's an apology pie. Vanilla cream with a cream cheese layer and cherry topping. Your favorite." I set it on the counter. Hattie had even written *Please forgive me* on top in whipped cream. "I'm sorry I kept things from Mike, and I'm sorry I kept things from you. You are my best friend and my sister, and he is my brother. I love you both and never meant to hurt you." I shoved the box even closer. She was looking at it but hadn't reached out for it yet. "I promise I won't keep things from either of you ever again." Even as I said it, I hoped this was a promise I really would be able to keep. "Can you please, please forgive me? I miss you so much. I don't want us to fight."

Bree wiped a tear from her cheek. "I don't want us to fight either."

I walked around the counter and hugged her. Thankfully, she hugged me back.

"I'm sorry too," Bree said. "I don't even know why I got so mad. You've kept things from Mike before, and I've even agreed that you should. I guess I was just hurt that you'd kept things from me. Important, life-changing information. I thought we told each other everything."

"We do. And I should have told you what I knew. I should have told both of you. I guess this was a secret I'd been keeping for so long, it was hard to let anyone in. But I know I should have. From now on, we're all in this together."

Bree hugged me again. A hard, long Bree hug and I knew things would be okay.

"Have you talked to Mike since I called him about the furniture store?"

She nodded. "I know you realized that something had been moved. We didn't talk long, but he needed to call to cancel our lunch date."

"I also spoke to Sue Wade, who told me that she had an idea about how to find and open the secret drawer in the desk we found. I called and spoke to Mike. I'm meeting him at his office at five. Maybe we can all have dinner after."

"That would be nice. I'll check with Mike when I'm done here for the day. And thanks for the pie."

I smiled and pulled on my mailbag. It might have been a good idea to say something more, but Bree was happy, and I didn't want to jinx things, so I waved and headed out the door.

Then I called Tony about dinner. I needed to check with Mike, but I really should check with Tony first. He suggested that we have Mike and Bree out to his place for dinner so we could talk and not worry about being overheard. He was already out there with the animals other than Tilly and assured me he had plenty of food to make something nice, so I texted Bree, and she agreed that a private conversation would be best. I was going to wait to talk to Mike, but I wanted to get our dinner plans settled, so I texted him as well, and he replied that dinner sounded nice.

For the first time in quite a while, I finally let myself believe that I could get my relationships back on track. Of course, I was still supposed to meet Mike in his office at five to try to open the desk, and I was going to have to hurry to get my route done on time. I stored my phone in my pocket and put my head down as I practically ran down the street. I knew that as long as I didn't make eye contact or stop to talk with anyone, I should be fine.

The more I thought about Jillian's description of the man who'd shown up at Star's shop, the more certain I was that I'd seen that man before. At Tony's, to be specific. It had been a while ago, before I'd share the truth about Dad with Mike, but I was pretty sure he was one of the men who'd stopped to talk to us in Tony's drive more than a year ago and warned us to back off from looking for my dad if we didn't want to get hurt.

Who was this guy, and why was he so invested in whatever was going on with my dad? I honestly didn't know if he was trying to help Dad by warning people away, or if he was the person who had been running around killing people who seemed to be associated with Dad. He could have just shot Tony and me if he wished us harm on the day he showed up rather than just warned us, but he hadn't. Maybe this guy was working with Dad as some sort of cleaner, and he only resorted to violence if he had to.

Or maybe the man Tony and I met over a year ago, the man Jillian saw at Star's store, and the man I saw shoot Star were different people. Tall and thin with dark hair really was a general sort of description.

As I'd hoped, the rest of my route went quickly. Mike wasn't back from the furniture store yet when Tilly and I arrived at his office, so we settled in to wait. Frank must have been with Mike because the only cop in the office was Gage, the new hire. I didn't want to cross the line by pumping him for information about the case, so I settled on a discussion about the pending storm and how it might affect the weekend event.

Fortunately, Mike and Frank showed up shortly. Frank made a comment about comparing the prints they'd found on the picture frame with the ones found in Star's store as well as the ones found on the desk. There were prints everywhere that could be processed, but I suspected they might be looking for a specific set of prints.

"So, you think you might know how to find the secret compartment in the desk?" Mike asked.

"Sue had an idea of what type of desk it was and how to open it. I figured it wouldn't hurt to give it a try."

"I agree." Mike headed down the hallway to the evidence room, where he'd stored the desk. "So, what do we do?"

"According to Sue, there will be a small knob in the back of the center drawer."

Mike reached his hand inside and began feeling around.

"She said it won't seem like much, but once you find the knob, you turn it all the way to the left as far as it will go and then give the knob a little tug, and a latch of sorts should appear at the back of the desk."

Mike did as I instructed, and he found a knob.

"Well, would you look at that?" Mike said. "What do we do now?"

"Give the latch a pull, and a panel on the back should pop open."

Mike did as instructed, and the secret compartment appeared.

"I have to admit that is pretty cool," Mike said.

I looked in the compartment. "It is, but it's empty."

"So it is." Mike sighed. "I wonder if this compartment was empty all along, or if it originally contained something that Star and Colton found and moved."

"I don't see how we can know now," I answered.

Chapter 13

Mike headed home to pick up Bree, and I drove to Tony's. By the time Tilly and I arrived, Tony had seasoned some delicious-looking filets that he planned to top with a rich Burgundy sauce. He was also going to serve garlic mashed potatoes, asparagus, and a nice green salad with his homemade dressing. I know I say this a lot, but I really did consider myself lucky that I'd found a boyfriend who could cook.

"Mike called. They should be here in about twenty minutes," Tony informed me after kissing me hello.

"Okay. I'm going to run upstairs to change." I bent down to pick up Tang, who was crawling up my leg. "Is there anything we should discuss before they get here? Anything you found out that you might want to run past me first?"

"No. Everything I'd dug up can be discussed with us all. I'll feed Tilly while you are changing. I've already fed the others."

I know it was crazy that I should be feeling nervous about having dinner with Mike and Bree, but I really wanted things to go well. I was tired of being at odds with them, and now that they'd both opened the door to a resumption of our previous relationship, I just hoped I didn't open my mouth and ruin everything. I wasn't sure that anything I'd found out today would help Mike with his investigation, but having news to share did seem like a good excuse to get together.

By the time I made it back downstairs, Mike and Bree had arrived, and Tony was pouring wine for everyone. I took a deep breath and plastered on a smile as I walked into the kitchen, where Mike and Bree were sitting at the counter, watching Tony finish preparing our meal. Mike had been telling Tony about the fingerprint he'd found on the frame of the painting that had been left leaning on the wall. I knew that Frank had been looking for a match when I'd left Mike's office after opening the desk, but I'd never heard what he'd found.

Tony smiled at me as he handed me a wineglass. "Mike was just telling me that he found a print on the painting in the furniture store that matches one found on the counter of the antique store, but they don't match any print in the system."

"There must be a lot of people who don't have prints on file unless they have a job that requires printing or they have been arrested at some point in their life," I said.

"It is true that we pull a lot of prints with no matches," Mike agreed. "Some states require prints to be provided when getting a driver's license, but Montana is not one of them." He took a sip of his wine. "The reality is that given the fact that Colton and Star both sold used and antique furniture, it seems likely they had a lot of the same customers; however, it is unlikely that most customers had any reason to leave a print on a huge painting that was hanging on a wall unless they were the one to take it down from the wall. I really think that print could be important, so I told Frank to increase the search parameters."

"If the person who took the painting off the wall was looking for something, which seems likely, maybe we will find that it is that same person who is responsible for both murders," Bree said.

"That's what I'm hoping," Mike said. "Even though the secret compartment in the desk that Tess and I found was empty, that doesn't mean that something wasn't in there at one point, or that someone didn't have reason to believe that whoever owned the desk before it was sold didn't leave something there."

"Like what?" Bree asked.

"I have no idea," Tony said, "but perhaps there was a land deed that showed property lines to be other than are currently believed or a birth certificate that showed someone's ancestry was not what they'd been told. Or perhaps there were bonds of some sort in the desk or stock certificates that could be worth millions."

"Or proof of a crime or perhaps proof of an inheritance, such as a never-found last will and testament," I added.

"Let's face it," Mike said. "The concept of hidden documents provides a range of motives. If any such documents ever existed and were once hidden in the desk's compartment, we need to find them, although it will be doubly hard to find them because we don't even know what we are looking for."

"Did you ever get into Colton's safe? The one we found in his office at the furniture store?" I asked.

"I did," Mike answered. "There was money and some files pertaining to items he'd recently purchased, but nothing that jumped out as a motive."

"What about the desk?" I asked. "Was the paperwork for the desk inside the safe?"

"It was not," Mike answered. "Star might have had it, or it could be stashed with whatever might have been found in the desk."

"What do we know about the previous owner of the desk?" I asked.

Tony jumped in. "The desk was purchased from the estate of a man named Graham Beaumont. Mr. Beaumont died this past summer, and his estate was divided between his surviving children, who seemed to only be interested in the cash, because the man's home, his vehicles, and the furnishings, books, and household items in the home were all either sold at auction or in the estate sale." Tony took a breath and then continued. "Mr. Beaumont was in his nineties and had lived on the estate for about thirty years. Before that, he lived and worked on a ranch just south of Wolf Creek."

"Do we know when he purchased the desk or whom he purchased it from?" I asked.

"I was unable to find proof of where the desk came from, but I suspect it might have come to Montana through Graham's wife, Annalise, who was born and raised in Washington, DC. She met Graham while he was attending college in Baltimore. From what I could find, Annalise came from money, and I believe that it was her money that allowed Graham to purchase the estate he retired to."

"So if the desk was from Colonial times, whatever was hidden in the desk could have been put there just prior to the man's death or more than two hundred years ago," Bree said.

"Theoretically, yes," Tony agreed.

"Did you ever get hold of the woman whose number you identified early on?" Bree asked Tony. "I've forgotten her name."

"Celia Bronson," Tony answered. "And yes, I was able to track her down. She heard about the desk and was interested in obtaining it for her own collection. She said she spoke to Star initially, but after she died, she contacted Colton, which is why there were calls from her to both of them."

"We found the desk in Colton's barn, so we know she didn't purchase it from him. Did you feel there was any reason to suspect that she might have killed two people in her effort to obtain the desk?" I asked.

"Not at all," Tony answered. "The woman did seem very interested in buying the desk, but I didn't pick up the obsessive killer vibe from her."

"So, what now?" Bree asked.

"I have one other lead that may or may not turn out to be relevant," I added. "I spoke to Jillian from the pharmacy today, and she told me that she was in Star's shop when a man dressed in a suit came in and kicked her out." I went on to describe exactly what had occurred.

"Tall with dark hair does tend to be a common variable," Mike agreed. "But that still isn't enough. A lot of men are tall with dark hair."

"I never did see the face of the man who shot Star, but Jillian seemed to get a pretty good look at the one who came to Star's store. You'll want to talk to her personally to see if you can home in on some distinguishing features."

"Is it possible that there is more than one thing going on here?" Tony asked.

"What do you mean?" Mike asked in return.

"We know that Star had been digging around in her past and that she inadvertently found herself mixed up with Grant Tucker and whatever occurred at the time of her mother's death. We have speculated that her digging around into the past of a man who clearly wants to disappear could be what got her killed, and it does seem as if the man who came to see her in the shop before her death had features similar to the man who warned us off as well as the man who pulled Mike aside at the restaurant more than a year ago. But even if we assume that the one who stopped in at the antique store to speak to Star is the same one who showed up at my house to warn me off and is also the same one who pulled Mike aside at the restaurant to warn him off, that doesn't mean he is the person who shot both Star and Colton."

"Wait," Bree said. "Are you saying that while the man who visited Star at the antique store may be the same person who was running interference for your dad all along, that doesn't mean he is the one who shot her?"

"Exactly," Tony confirmed. "It seems feasible that Star could have been shot by the man who seems to be running interference for Mike and Tess's dad, but why would this person shoot Colton?"

"So you think that the fact that Star was looking into her past is nothing more than a coincidence and had nothing to do with her death?" I clarified.

"Perhaps," Tony answered.

"That would be just too bizarre," Bree said.

"I agree," Mike said. "Until we find the killer, we can't know for certain what the motive for the deaths might have been, but I've had Tony do a thorough investigation into Colton's last days, and he found no evidence that Colton knew anything about our father or Star's past, so it seems unlikely that her past had anything to do with the murders."

We fell into silence. Eventually, Tony said, "Dinner is ready. We can talk while we eat, but it seems to me that the answer to everything most likely will be found in some documents that might have been hidden in the desk. That is the only thing that makes any sense to me at this point."

Chapter 14

Friday, December 20

It came to me in the middle of the night, the idea that perhaps Star had stashed the documents she and Colton had found in the safest place she could think of, her safety deposit box. I knew she had one because that was where she'd told me she'd stashed the envelope with the information about her parents that Sam Denton had compiled and left for her with a friend. When I'd asked Mike about it early on, he'd said that he would need a court order to get into the box, but that was two weeks ago, so chances were he'd made progress on that front. I'd need to ask him about it when I saw him today.

In the meantime, I had a very long day to prepare for. I had my usual mail route to complete, and then I was going to meet Tony at the opening of the carnival, which was set up the day before. The sky was dark, and snow was falling gently. The high temperatures were forecast to be in the mid-twenties for both today and tomorrow, with nighttime lows in the single digits. I didn't think anyone would show up for the outdoor rides that were scheduled to be open from three to nine p.m. today and from ten a.m. to nine p.m. tomorrow and Sunday.

"Be sure to wear lots of layers," Tony counseled as he handed me a cup of coffee.

"I have a bag with extra hats, gloves, sweaters, and socks too. I'll leave it in the truck, along with my heavy boots and my extra jacket in case the one I wear for work today gets too wet. This whole Christmas carnival idea was nuts."

"I agree. Your mom agrees. The entire Christmas on Main committee agrees, but the event planner signed the contract, so even though she is no longer in the picture, the town is on the hook for it." Tony looked out the window. I followed his gaze. It seemed as if the snow was coming down harder.

"Hopefully, the committee plans to bring the craft and food vendors inside," I said.

"When I spoke to your mother yesterday, she indicated as much."

Tony handed me a muffin and an apple for my drive into town.

"I should go," I said. "I'll text you later, so we can figure out a place to meet up."

"Maybe you should leave Tilly with me today. You won't have anything to do with her after work if you take her."

I knew Tony was right, but I was going to miss having my copilot today. I could drop her at my cabin after work, but all the other animals were here at

Tony's, so she'd be alone while we were at the carnival. In the long run, she really would be better off hanging back here with the others today.

I decided to start my route in the middle so I could talk to Mike about the safety deposit box first thing. Thankfully, when I arrived at his office, he was there and didn't seem all that busy.

"After you and Bree left last night, I got to thinking about the safety deposit box Star told me she had, where she stored the envelope I delivered to her. I wondered if perhaps items from the secret drawer in the desk might be in there as well."

"I actually thought of that too and was able to finally get permission to get into it. The bank manager and I opened it before the bank opened."

"And?"

"And it was empty. The manager checked the log, and it showed that Star accessed the box earlier on the day she died."

I narrowed my gaze. "She must have emptied it, but why?"

Mike slowly shook his head. "I have no idea, but the fact that she emptied her box hours before she was killed seems significant to me."

"I agree. And we know that she closed her shop on the day she died as well. It looks like she felt she needed to take care of whatever was in the file."

"But why right then?"

"Maybe the guy who came to see her when Jillian was in the store threatened to harm her if she didn't turn over the information she received that related to her parents. Maybe she decided that it was in her own best interest to turn the envelope over to him, so she went to the bank to get it, although I have no idea why she would have moved whatever stuff might have been hidden in the desk."

"Maybe there never was anything in the desk after all, and even if there was something, maybe she hadn't put it in her safety deposit box," Mike said.

"I guess that could be, but she told me that she put the envelope I delivered to her in the box, so we can at least assume she took that out when she went to the box the day she died. If nothing else, I feel like we should figure out what happened to it."

"If Star did retrieve the packet to give to someone who was threatening her, whatever was in it is most likely long gone," Mike pointed out.

"Well, that's frustrating."

"It is," Mike agreed. "I guess at this point, all we can do is try to think like Star to figure out where she would have put important papers if she didn't, in fact, turned them over to someone who might have been threatening her."

That was a question that would haunt me all day as I went about my route. I really, really wanted to find the envelope that Denton had gathered about Dad, and I also felt that if there had been something hidden in the back of the desk, something that someone was after, that was most likely the motive for both Star and Colton's deaths. Of course, even if there had been documents and they had been hidden away, I had no idea where to look for them that we hadn't already looked. Star had died a week before Colton, so it made sense that if he knew where the documents were hidden and how to get to them, he would have retrieved them at some point during that week. He must have known that Star's belongings would be inspected with a fine-tooth comb during the investigation into her murder, so it made sense to me that he would have retrieved anything that existed and then hidden them somewhere he felt was secure.

I thought about his house, his workroom, and his furniture store. It made the most sense to me that he would hide something important in his house, where he could keep a close eye on it. But where? Mike, Bree, Tony, and I had looked all over the place. Mike and Bree had searched Colton's home office, but perhaps they'd missed something. I needed to get my route done, but this was important, too, so I headed toward Mike's office once again.

"So, what do you think?" I asked after I explained my logic to Mike.

"I guess it wouldn't hurt to take a second look."

"I would help you, but I'm already behind on my route, and this is a Friday, so I want to get everything delivered before the businesses begin closing for the weekend, and Bree is working as well. Perhaps Tony can help you."

"I'll call him."

I had to admit that it almost killed me to bow out of the hunt, but I did have a responsibility to deliver the mail in a timely manner, and it was a responsibility I took seriously. Mike picked up the phone and called Tony while I was still there. They agreed to meet at Colton's place, and I went back out into the snow to complete my route. Sometimes doing the responsible thing was no fun at all. If it had been any day other than a Friday, I might have taken the risk of not finishing in time and delivered the things I hadn't gotten to with the next day's mail. But this was a weekend, and there was a lot of holiday mail, so I knew a late delivery would not go over well with my customers.

By the time I wrapped up my route with Sisters' Diner, I was wet and cold and pretty grumpy. Neither Mike nor Tony had called me or returned the calls I'd made to them. I wasn't at all happy about being excluded.

"Hey, Aunt Ruthie," I said, setting a pile of mail on the counter. The restaurant was closed by now, but Ruthie was still on the premises cleaning up. "Is Mom over at the carnival?"

"She is. They went ahead and opened it despite the weather. I suppose there are folks in town who will show up, no matter the cold and snow. It isn't windy at least, so that helps. But according to my weather app, the storm that is south of us is heading in this direction now. From my calculations, it should be here by midnight. I doubt the carnival will be able to operate tomorrow."

"Is it supposed to dump a lot of snow on us?" I asked.

"Several feet. If we get too much too fast, it won't be only the carnival that will be impacted but the entire event. If the roads are closed, the tourists from the neighboring towns won't be able to get here, and if they can't get here, the whole thing really will be a bust."

"I'm sure Mom is at the end of her rope."

"And how," Ruthie agreed. "If you are headed over to the carnival to help out, you might want to tread lightly. I'm afraid your mom has been snapping at everyone today."

"Thanks for the warning. I'm going to change out of my uniform and then head over. You haven't seen or heard from either Mike or Tony this afternoon, have you?"

She shook her head. "No. Neither came in or called."

"They were working on something together, but they aren't answering my calls. I'm starting to get a little bit worried."

"The storm is messing with the cell reception. I'm sure they're fine. You might want to check with Bree to see if she's heard from Mike." Ruthie glanced at the clock. "She is probably still at the bookstore."

"That's a good idea. I'll head in that direction."

Bree's store was closed, but like Ruthie, she was still there, cleaning up before leaving for the day. I knocked on the door, and she let me in.

"Hey, Tess. Where's Tilly?"

"At Tony's with the rest of the animals. We are supposed to meet up and head over to the carnival, but I haven't heard from him all afternoon."

She frowned. "Yeah, Mike hasn't returned my text either. I hope everything is okay."

"I'm sure it is. They were heading over to Colton's house to take another look around his home office. I wouldn't think that would take all that long, but maybe they found what they were looking for and followed up on it. I think I might take a run over to Colton's to see if they are still there. Do you want to come with me?"

"I do. Just give me a minute to lock everything up."

Chapter 15

When Bree and I arrived at Colton's house, we found both Mike's cruiser and Tony's truck in the drive. The house was dark, with the exception of a single light at the back.

"I can't believe they are still here," I said. "They were supposed to meet up with each other hours ago."

Bree opened the passenger door to my Jeep; I'd offered to drive. I unclipped my seat belt and got out as well.

"I hope everything is okay," Bree said.

"I'm sure it is, but keep your eyes open just in case."

She swallowed hard and nodded. I took the lead, and she fell in behind me. When we arrived at the front door, I opened it and called out, "Mike! Tony!"

"Back here," both replied.

Well, at least they sounded okay. Bree and I headed down the hallway. I gasped when I arrived at the office to find both Mike and Tony tied to chairs.

"What happened?" I asked as I began untying Tony, and Bree began untying Mike.

"There was someone here when we arrived," Mike began. "They'd parked around back, so we didn't see the car. They took us by surprise."

"They had a gun," Tony added. "They had me tie Mike up, and then the guy tied me up while the woman held a gun on us."

"Thank God all they did was tie you up," Bree said as she stepped back, and Mike stood up.

"When I first realized we weren't alone, I thought we were dead." Mike pulled Bree into his arms. I could see that the experience had shaken him, although he was trying to appear calm.

"But the woman just told Mike to drop his gun and then they tied us up and left," Tony said as I finally got the rope around his feet loose and he stood as well.

"Do you know who it was?" I asked.

"The pair wore masks, so I didn't see the face of either individual, but Tony said he recognized the woman's voice," Mike answered.

"Who was it?" I asked.

"Celia Bronson," Tony answered.

"The woman who tried to buy the desk from Star first and then Colton?" I asked.

Tony nodded. "I've spoken to her on the phone twice. She has a way of rolling her Rs. I'm sure the woman today was the one I've spoken to on the phone."

"Do you think they are the ones who killed Star and Colton?" I wondered.

"I don't," Mike said. "I think if the pair we stumbled upon had already killed two people, they probably wouldn't have hesitated to kill us. I didn't get the feeling they wanted to hurt anyone. I think they were here looking for something, and then we showed up. They probably saw us through the window and had time to get into place before we entered the office. They were on us before I had any idea that anyone was already here."

"So they either must have been looking for the desk or for whatever they believed was in the secret compartment," Bree said.

"I think we will find that Ms. Bronson and her partner in crime are the ones who broke into the furniture store as well," Tony added. "All we need to do now is to compare the prints on the gun with the ones on the picture frame."

I noticed Tony glancing at Mike's gun, which had been left on the desk. "She picked it up?" I asked.

Tony nodded. "The man told Mike to drop his gun, and he set it on the floor and kicked it forward, and then the woman picked it up and put it on the desk. She was not wearing gloves."

Mike used a towel he found in the bathroom to pick up and wrap the gun so as not to smear any prints that might have been left.

"So, what now?" I asked. "Did you see the car they were driving?"

"We didn't," Mike answered. "But Tony is pretty sure the woman is Celia Bronson, so I have a place to start. I'm going to head back to the office to run the prints on the gun just to be sure. Once I've done that, I'll pay a visit to Ms. Bronson."

"And we should get over to the carnival," I said to Tony. "Assuming you aren't injured in any way."

"I'm fine. And your mom will be frantic by now, I'm sure."

I looked at Bree. "Do you want to come with us?"

"You guys go ahead. I'll stay with Mike."

"We never did look for the documents we hoped to find," Tony reminded Mike.

"Maybe we can come back later. I'll call you."

Tony agreed, and we all headed out to the drive. I planned to drop off the Jeep at my cabin and then head into town with Tony. It was a good thing all the animals were safe and comfortable at Tony's. I had a feeling this was going to be a long night.

******

When we arrived at the carnival, we found it packed with locals and tourists alike. I guess I was somewhat surprised by how crowded it was, given the fact that it had been snowing off and on all day. Of course, today's snow was the gentle sort that fluttered around a bit but didn't amount to much when it came to overall accumulation. The overnight forecast was still calling for precipitation that would be measured in feet. If that occurred, I was pretty sure the carnival would be over almost before it got started.

"I have to say, the place feels festive," I said to Tony.

He grinned. "It really does. If not for the fact that we promised your mom we'd help out, I'd buy a roll of game tickets. Where are we supposed to meet her anyway?"

I pulled my phone out of my pocket. "I'm not sure. I wasn't expecting this crowd and figured we'd just look around for her. I'll text her to see where she is."

As it turned out, Mom was in the ticket booth, so we took off in that direction. I hoped she'd ended up with enough other volunteers; Tony and I had both fallen down on the job. Not that we didn't have a good excuse for being late, but Mom had been so stressed all week that I'd wanted to be there for her.

"Hi, Mom, sorry we're late." I offered the woman who'd given birth to me a warm hug.

"I was wondering what had happened to the two of you."

"We were helping Mike," I explained. "But we're here now if you need us."

Mom glanced out toward the rides. "Actually, I seem to have plenty of volunteers tonight. Tomorrow may be another story altogether unless the snow we are expecting actually shows up, in which case there may be nothing to volunteer for."

I looked up toward the sky. "It's not too bad right now."

"Let's hope it stays that way." Mom paused as a woman with three children came up to buy three wristbands that allowed for unlimited rides for the evening. "So, you're helping Mike with his murder cases?" she asked after the woman and her children left.

"Sort of. We helped him to open the secret compartment in the desk at the center of whatever was going on with Star and Colton."

"Did you find anything that would point to a motive?"

I shook my head. "It was empty. But Mike has some new evidence he is working on, so we might have some answers by tomorrow." I decided not to mention that Mike and Tony had been left tied up in Colton's house. Mom was stressed enough as it was. "We're going to meet him later to go over a few things."

"I'm glad the two of you are getting along. A mother doesn't like it when her children are at odds."

Tony and I hung out for a while, mostly just to enjoy the festive atmosphere. If the storm did blow in as expected, tonight could end up being both the first and the last night of the event. After we'd eaten some junk food and played a few games, I called Mike, who informed me that he'd arrested Celia Bronson and her brother for trespassing and accosting a police officer. As we suspected, Celia was after an old deed that she believed had been stored in the desk. Mike promised to tell me the whole story later, but he needed to get off the phone right away. Before he hung up, though, I asked if he thought Celia and her brother had shot Star and Colton, and he said that he was fairly certain that he was back to square one on that particular question.

Tony and I decided to head out to his place. It was late, and we were tired, and the thought of snuggling up with the animals in front of the fire seemed too good to resist.

Chapter 16

Saturday, December 21

By the time the alarm clock went off the next morning, we were blanketed in a layer of snow that was going to take some serious shoveling to dig out from. Mom called to let us know that the carnival portion of the event was canceled for the day, but she hoped to dig everything out so it could reopen tomorrow. The craft and food vendors were warm and cozy in the community center, and the local snowplow drivers were busy clearing the town streets so that those who were inclined to head into town would be able to do so.

Given the fact that Tony lived up on the mountain, we figured we wouldn't see a plow for at least a day, so we reconciled ourselves to settling in and enjoying the first major snowstorm of the season.

"I spoke to Mike," Tony informed me as he slipped a breakfast casserole into the oven.

"Oh. What did he have to say?"

"Apparently, Celia Bronson's grandfather was one of the first people to settle in White Eagle. He carved out a large ranch for himself that he handed down to his two sons, who divided the land rather than running it together. At the time the ranch was divided, a map was drawn with borders clearly marked so each son would know what land belonged to him and what belonged to his brother. Over the years, the property lines blurred until a major dispute between two present heirs, Celia's brother and their uncle's oldest son, Seth, erupted. Celia felt it important to track down the original map and document that described the split, but she couldn't find it. Eventually, she remembered her grandmother's desk with the secret compartment."

"I wonder why she thought the documents would be in the desk."

"Her grandmother had once mentioned to her that all her most important documents were in that compartment, so Celia thought that perhaps the map and land deed were there as well. The problem was that her mother hadn't liked the desk, and when she inherited it, she sold it. Celia spent a lot of time tracking the desk down, but by the time she'd traced it to Graham Beaumont, he'd passed away, and all his possessions had been sold off. Celia was able to determine that Star was the one who'd bought the desk, so she called her and offered to buy it. Star told her that she was the second person to call about the desk, and while she and her partner planned to sell it eventually, they weren't ready to do it quite yet."

"So I'm assuming it was Celia who told Star about the secret compartment?"

"It was, but she didn't tell her how to access it, only that it existed, and that she would be willing to pay her simply to look inside the hidden panel for a document she believed belonged to her. While Star was mulling this over, someone else apparently called with a similar request. According to Celia, she said that she needed to speak to her partner and would get back to her, but Star was shot and killed before she was able to return Celia's call."

"So Celia sought out Colton," I assumed.

"Yes. At some point, Celia found out who Star's partner was, so when she learned that Star was dead, she called Colton and once again offered to buy the desk. Colton wasn't ready to sell the desk but agreed to call her when he was."

"Colton probably realized that the reason Star had been shot and killed could very well be due to whatever was in the desk so many people seemed to want."

Tony nodded. "I suspect that is true. Also, keep in mind that when Star was shot, she had already cleaned out her safety deposit box. We are assuming that means that she was able to access the hidden compartment in the desk and that she had initially stashed whatever was inside it in her safety deposit box, but then thought better of keeping it there for some reason."

"What reason? What could be safer than a safety deposit box?"

Tony shrugged. "I don't know. What we do know is that by the time we found the desk, it was empty, and when Mike checked the safety deposit box, it was empty as well. We still have a lot of blanks that need to be filled in."

I took a sip of my coffee. "Okay, in summary, we know Celia desperately wanted the map and deed to the land, which she believed was stored in the desk by her grandmother. She figured out who the desk had been sold to and tracked him down, but he had died. She then traced the desk to Star and offered to buy it. When Star was killed, she sought out Colton, and when he was killed, she broke into his store and his home, looking for the map and deed she needed."

"That seems to sum up what we know or suspect at this point. Celia told Mike that she had broken into Star's home and business as well, but she never found what she was looking for."

"Because it wasn't there," I said. "I mean, if you think about it, we looked and looked and didn't find anything like the map and deed Celia says she is looking for. Sure, we didn't know exactly what we were looking for at that time, but I think an old map and deed would have stood out as being relevant if we'd come across them."

"I agree. So the question is, where are the map and deed, and where is the envelope Star received from Denton's friend?"

Boy, did I wish I had the answer to those questions.

Tony got up to check the casserole, and I refilled both our mugs with coffee. It had stopped snowing, although it was still overcast. According to the weather report, the storm had moved on, and we were expecting fairly mild weather for Sunday.

"So if Celia is behind the break-ins at the furniture store and Colton's house, and she is not responsible for either murder, who is?" I asked.

"Another good question." Tony headed to the refrigerator to pull out a fruit salad he must have prepared while I was still upstairs.

"We have the man who kicked Jillian out of Star's store, who may or may not be associated with my dad or whatever is going on regarding him. He seemed like the cold blooded sort who would walk up to someone's door and shoot them."

"I agree. He does make a good candidate. But there are others."

"Such as?" I asked.

"Celia's brother is in a land dispute with another relative. We also suspect that Star told Celia that someone else was also interested in the desk. It seems possible that this other someone could have approached the situation a bit more forcefully than Celia did."

"I suppose that is true. We should try to find out who the other person interested in the desk actually was."

"Mike might know," Tony answered. He pulled on a pair of mitts and reached into the oven for the casserole. It looked delicious. Nice and cheesy, with egg, bacon, onion, and spinach.

Once we'd eaten and cleaned up the kitchen, Tony and I headed outside with shovels and the snowblower. It took us three hours to clear the walks, driveway, patio, and decks. A plow would come by at some point to clear the streets, but for now, we were snowed in.

As soon as we'd finished shoveling, we decided to take a spa. There was something wonderful about sitting outside in a tub full of hot water while jets hit your back as snow flurries caressed your face.

"By the way, how did Shaggy's meeting with the video game company go?" I asked, as my mind wandered from one random subject to the next. Shaggy was Tony's best friend, and the two of them had been working together to develop a new game. They had a prototype ready for testing, and Tony had told me that Shaggy had meetings set up with several distributors.

"All the meetings have gone well," Tony answered. "I think we will have more than one company willing to make an offer, which means that we should get top dollar."

I leaned my head back against the headrest as the water bubbled all around me. "That's wonderful. I bet Shaggy is over the moon."

"He is. He's even talking about using part of his portion of the profit to expand his store."

Shaggy owned a store that sold video games and comic books.

"And what are you going to do with your share?" I asked. Tony already had a lot of money, so the profit from the game wouldn't affect his lifestyle as much as it would Shaggy's.

"Actually, I am going to donate my profit to the shelter."

I opened my eyes and sat up. "The shelter? You mean the animal shelter?"

Tony nodded. "I've spoken to Brady about it." Brady was the local veterinarian and owner of the only animal shelter in town. "I really love the ideas the two of you have for not only expanding the training facility but for offering a permanent residence for senior dogs and cats and other hard-to-place pets. Brady and I went over some designs he's been playing around with but didn't think the budget would support. With the proceeds from the game, he should be able to do everything he can imagine."

I let out a little screech of happiness and moved onto Tony's lap. I put my arms around his neck and kissed him. "I love you. And not just because you are making my dreams come true as well as Brady's, but because of your big heart."

He smiled and kissed me back. "I love you too, and not just because you are sitting on my lap, which is giving me all sorts of ideas."

Chapter 17

Quite a while later, Tony called Mike about some ideas he'd had regarding the research he was helping him with. I was trying very hard not to insert myself into the situation and take over completely, but that didn't mean that I wasn't listening with both ears. Tony had filled me in on most of this already, but I was still interested in the direction the conversation would head once Mike had a chance to give his feedback.

"I found out that Ivana Kowalski first worked for Layton Henderson in his import-export business," Tony said into the phone. "About eight months before she became pregnant and ran away, she was transferred to his facility in Hungary, which presently deals with artificial intelligence but at that time dealt with the manipulation of human intelligence utilizing a variety of methods. We knew that and have discussed it before. What we didn't know prior to my research yesterday is that after Ivana became pregnant facility, we assume without permission to ᴄegan using the name Polly Davis. She ⌐ ᴛo the United States using the Polly Davis alias, as a guest of Grant Tucker, who, interestingly enough, was Henderson's head of security prior to running off with Ivana."

I couldn't hear Mike's response because Tony had not put the phone on Speaker, but from the long silence on Tony's end of the conversation, it seemed apparent that Mike had quite a lot to say about the situation. When Tony had first told me that Grant Tucker had worked for Henderson in a very high-ranking position, I'd been surprised as well. What could have led our dad to turn his back on his boss and run off with one of his assets? Had Dad been in love with Ivana, or had he simply befriended her because he felt sorry for her? I supposed this was a question we would never know the answer to. The other answer we might never know was who Grant Tucker was before he began working for Henderson. According to Tony, he wasn't anywhere on any radar, nor did he have a paper trail until shortly before taking the job with Henderson. It was Tony's theory that Dad might have been deep undercover when he'd hooked up with Henderson to find out what he was doing with his human test subjects. I supposed that fit what we suspected: that at some point, my father had been CIA or a member of some other supersecret agency. If he had taken on the name Grant Tucker to go undercover, I had to wonder who the man I'd called Dad was before taking on all the aliases.

"No, I don't have proof that your dad was undercover for a government organization while he worked for Henderson, though the theory does fit what we know about him to date," Tony said, answering a question Mike must have asked.

"Yes, it is possible that Star was killed because of the information contained in the file she received if the person who killed her believed she had read all the paperwork and had the potential to do something with it," Tony said after a brief pause to listen to Mike's reply.

It had occurred to me many times in the past weeks that if we wanted to figure out who, if anyone, might want to kill Star because of the file, we needed to figure out exactly what was in it.

"Yes, I have considered that," Tony said.

Considered what? I wondered. Listening in on half the conversation wasn't turning out to be as informative as I'd hoped.

"I have a theory, but at this point, all it is is a theory," Tony said. "We suspect that Star and Colton found the hidden panel and everything that was stored in it. We also suspect that initially, Star put the items she found in the desk in her safety deposit box, along with the file that she had obtained from Denton's friend." Tony paused; I supposed Mike might have said something. Then he went on. "Yes, we are aware that on the day she died, Star went into the bank to access her safety deposit box, and we assume she took everything that was in it with her when she left because the box is empty now. What if Colton noticed the envelope Star received from Denton's friend when she showed up with the items she found in the desk, and what if, when she died, Colton not only took everything that had been hidden in the desk but the envelope as well?"

Wow. Tony pretty effectively had figured out a way to link Colton into the whole thing if it was someone connected to Star and her past that had killed him. If Colton was able to take possession of the envelope, maybe he did something that alerted whoever had killed Star that he had it, which was what led to his own death. I had to hand it to Tony; he really was a genius.

Of course, in this case, I found myself hoping he was wrong. It was horrible that two people were dead no matter what the reason, but the idea that their deaths could somehow be linked with my father and his covert activities left me with a rumbling feeling in my stomach. Of course, this was the theory I'd been working off of all along, so I wasn't sure why I was surprised it was all coming together.

"I have a thought," I said.

Tony glanced at me and then told Mike to hang on for a moment. "Is it something you want me to mention to Mike?"

I nodded. "While I was sitting here listening to you talking to Mike, the idea popped into my head that the fingerprints on the 'open' and 'closed' sign at Star's shop might have the fingerprints of the man who kicked Jillian out. I know the store is a public place and there will be way too many prints found within the interior to home in on any one set, but who other than Star, who ran the shop without any employees, would be flipping the sign back and forth?"

"Hang on," Tony said. He put his phone on Speaker. "Tell Mike what you just said to me."

I did, and Mike agreed that the sign might provide a clean set of prints. Jillian had specifically said that the man in the suit who had kicked her out of the store had flipped the sign from "open" to "closed" himself. We all agreed it was certainly worth taking a look. Mike and Bree lived in town and were not snowed in, so he would be able to head to Star's store to retrieve the sign.

After he signed off, Tony and I discussed several options for the day. It was a good day to stay in, but part of me felt a lot more isolated than my busy mind wanted to accept.

"I'm going to log on and check my emails while we figure out what to do next," Tony said.

"I should check mine as well. I haven't even logged on for a couple of days."

We both picked up our laptops and settled in at the table in front of the fireplace.

"That's odd," Tony said.

"What is?" I asked.

"I have an email, and the entire body of it is two words, a name actually."

That had my interest. "What name?"

"Darwin Norlander."

"Who is Darwin Norlander?" I wondered.

"I have no idea. Nor can I tell immediately who sent it. I'm going downstairs where I can take a closer look with my large computers."

I folded up my laptop. "I'll come with you."

Tony went straight to one of his workstations and began to type. I sat down in one of the chairs he'd provided for the times when I joined him there, a comfy one that reclined, so I settled in, reopened my laptop, and went back to my own emails.

After a while, Tony said, "Darwin Norlander was an associate of Layton Henderson. In fact, it appears he was one of the few considered to be a member of his inner circle."

"Was?" I asked.

"According to the information I have been able to dig up, it appears that Norlander and Henderson parted ways maybe six or eight months ago."

"Okay, that could be important. Who sent you the email with the name?" I asked.

"I have no idea. I've tried to backtrack and trace the source, but I'm being blocked at every turn. Whoever sent the email wanted me to have the man's name but did not want to be found or identified."

"My dad?"

"Perhaps. I would think that, given his resources, he knows exactly what is going on in White Eagle."

I got up from the chair and walked across the room. I stood behind Tony. "So, what are you going to do?"

Tony pulled up a photo. "This is Darwin Norlander. Could he be the man who shot Star?"

I looked carefully at the man in the photo. "Yes. That could be him. I didn't see the man's face, but he had dark hair like the man in the photo, and he was tall and thin, as it appears this man is." I put my hand on Tony's shoulder. "Is it possible my dad just handed us the killer?"

Tony minimized the photo and kept scrolling through a mass of code that I didn't recognize. "Maybe. Of course, we don't know for certain that the email came from your dad, and this isn't enough to prove this is the man who shot Star. And even if he is, we'll need to figure out whether he also shot Colton."

"How are we going to prove any of that?"

Tony paused and sat back in his chair. "I'm not sure yet. Right now, I'm trying to see if I can find out where in the world Darwin Norlander was during the eight days between Star and Colton's murder."

"We really need Star's file," I said.

"I agree, but it seems possible to me that the file is long gone. If we find it, great, but we need to work on finding our answers another way." Tony turned his attention back to the computer. "I want to check out a few things. Can you run upstairs and call Mike? Tell him about the email and let him know I'll call him if I find something important."

"Okay. I can do that. I'll be back down when I'm done."

The secure room downstairs had no cell service, so I understood why Tony couldn't call Mike himself without having to stop what he was doing, but I still found myself hoping that my being the one to call wouldn't send the wrong message.

Thankfully, Mike seemed fine with getting the call from me, and he was excited that we had a new lead that might have been provided by our father. I knew there was no way to know that for sure, but I suspected that both Mike and I secretly wanted some sort of proof that Dad was really a good guy, not some sort of monster.

Chapter 18

The next several hours consisted of me waiting around and wondering while Tony focused all his attention on the task before him. Mike called me twice, which helped me to feel a bit more involved. The first call was to inform me that he had been able to lift a distinct set of prints from the store sign that did not match Star's. He was running them through the federal database. The second was to inform me that he'd shown a photo of Darwin Norlander to Jillian, who able to tell him definitively that he was not the person who had kicked her out of Star's store. That most likely meant the prints on the sign belonged to someone other than Norlander as well.

How many people were involved in this thing? I supposed the person who came to Star's store could have been one of the good guys, who'd shown up to warn her that the file she had in her possession put her in danger. She might even have gone to retrieve the file with the intention of getting rid of it. Of course, if that was the case, I wasn't sure how we'd know if she'd been successful in passing off the file or if she'd been shot before she could do anything with it. The fact that Colton died the following week indicated to me that if Star was killed at the hands of Darwin Norlander, Colton must have found the file and done something that landed him on Norlander's radar as well. Maybe he did a computer search that set off bells and whistles, or maybe if there was information about Henderson in the file, Colton had gone digging in all the wrong places.

The sun had already begun to work its way toward the horizon when Tony finally emerged from the computer room.

"What did you find?" I asked as soon as he had a chance to grab a beer and take a seat in the living room.

"Darwin Norlander passed through customs at LAX on December 4th. In Los Angeles, he boarded a plane to Denver International the following day, and Star was shot the day after that. I think it's very likely that he was the one who shot her."

I felt myself cringe. So her death was related to her past. When I'd found out about the desk, I'd hoped for a different ending. "And Colton?"

Tony paused before answering. "I'm not sure. He died a week later. The timeline doesn't make sense to me unless he didn't pop up as a threat on Norlander's radar until days after Star died."

"I can see that. If Star retrieved the file she had been sent by Denton's friend and hid it somewhere Colton would know about, it could have been a day or two before he went looking for it. Then he would have to read it and understand it enough to at least have some questions. I suppose he might have gone online at some point in an effort to find some answers and in doing so alerted whoever was monitoring things. Perhaps Norlander had left Montana but was still in the States, so when the alarm was sounded, he was sent back to take care of Colton as well."

"I suppose it could have happened that way."

"And the file?" I asked.

"I have no idea. We know that the man who shot Star went up to her house, killed her, and left. We don't know for certain that was the same thing that happened with Colton, but given where his body was found, it seems likely. Still, I suppose whoever shot him could have gone looking for the file and found it in his office or somewhere else in his home. Unless we find the file ourselves, which would prove that Star didn't hand it off and that it wasn't stolen from Colton, we may never know what happened to it."

"So, what now? How do we bring Norlander to justice, if he is, in fact, the one who shot two people?"

"Mike is calling a guy he knows at the FBI," Tony answered. "If Norlander is involved, this is something that needs to be investigated by someone with more resources than Mike has."

"Mike isn't going to bring up Dad?"

Tony shook his head. "No, he isn't. He wants to protect your dad as much as you do. He simply plans to say that an anonymous source brought up Norlander's name and then take it from there."

"Still, I have to admit to being worried. The feds are going to have questions that Mike isn't going to want to answer."

"If your dad is working for a government agency, as we suspect, chances are they already have the answers," Tony pointed out.

I supposed that much was true. I hoped we'd get some sort of resolution ourselves. If Star and Colton were killed by someone with international ties, it was highly unlikely that Mike would be the one to make the arrest or to close out the murder files for two people who'd been part of the White Eagle family.

"So, what is Mike's plan now?" I asked. Tony had been the last one to speak to him, so he knew more than I did. "If the feds agree to look into the murders, is Mike just going to stop looking for the killer? I mean, what if you two are wrong? What if Star and Colton were killed by a friend or a neighbor and not a thug working for a well-insulated billionaire?"

"I think that Mike plans to follow this through to the end. It may get even more confusing than it is right now if Henderson is behind everything, but keep in mind that it appears that Henderson and Norlander have parted ways. It might be possible that Norlander is working alone for some reason. Either way, I know that Mike wants real answers as much as we do."

"Yeah." I sighed. "I know." I glanced out the window at the falling snow. "I wonder how Mom is doing."

"Why don't you call her?"

I'd considered doing that, but the plow still hadn't been by, so it wasn't like Tony and I could help even if she was involved in some sort of crisis. Normally, Tony could get into town with his big four-wheel-drive truck despite the snow, but last night's storm had brought it down so hard and so fast that even larger vehicles weren't getting through.

"I'll try to call the county to see if I can find out when the plow might come by," Tony offered. "I should have called earlier, but I became preoccupied once I noticed the email."

"That's understandable. If you think a call would help get them here sooner, I think you should try. I do want to be there to support Mom if at all possible."

Tony made the call, and I went into the kitchen to scrounge up a snack. Tony had prepared a big breakfast, but I hadn't eaten all that much of it, and we never did have lunch. I was sorting through the contents of the refrigerator when I heard the familiar rumble of the snowplow. Ah, help had arrived at last. Maybe Tony and I would just head into town and have dinner there. After we checked in with Mom, of course.

"I was still on hold when I heard the plow, so I hung up," Tony said. "Should we head into town as soon as they make it through?"

"Let's. Maybe we should drop the animals off at my cabin. That way, if the snow comes back, we won't risk our being stuck in town while they are alone out here."

"Sounds like a plan. I'll start loading the truck."

Chapter 19

Monday, December 23

While Saturday was a bust for the carnival portion of Christmas on Main, the sun came out on Sunday, which allowed the rides to reopen for the day. With the warmer temps brought on by the clear and sunny day, it seemed that everyone who ventured out had a wonderful time. It might not have been the record-breaking event the committee had hoped for, but at least it wouldn't go down in history as a total loss either.

I couldn't believe it was already Christmas week. Christmas Eve dinner would be at Mom's and Christmas Day dinner this year would be at Mike and Bree's. Tony and I had decided to stay in town and hang out at my cabin on Christmas Eve after we got home from Mom's. We'd talked about heading out to his much more comfortable lake house, but the cabin was more convenient, and this year, I only had the one day off from work.

As for the murder investigations, Mike was working with the FBI, and I suspected the CIA was involved now as well. I didn't know that for certain, but it did seem like something bigger than two small-town murders was going on here. Given the complexity of the issues, I'd had to reconcile myself to the fact that we might never have all the answers we were seeking.

I planned to spend tonight at Tony's. Because we had family plans the next two nights, Tony and I had decided to have our couple's Christmas tonight. We were going to share a nice dinner and then, hopefully, a night of uninterrupted romance. With the stress of the past few weeks, I felt like some one-on-one time was definitely needed.

Thankfully, my day's route went faster than I'd expected. With the holiday fast approaching, I had another double-bag day with all the cards and gifts, but for the most part, folks along my route had customers to see to in their stores, shopping for those last-minute gifts, so I hadn't stopped to chat with them as I usually did.

It was dark by the time I made it out to Tony's. I was singing along with the songs on the Christmas station as I pulled into the driveway to find another car sitting in front of the house.

"Dark blue sedan," I said to Tilly.

I froze as I recognized the car in the drive. I couldn't be 100 percent sure this car was the same one the person who'd killed Star had been driving, but it looked pretty close to the same to me. The question was, what should I do? Head inside and check it out? Flee before I was noticed?

Making a decision, I turned off my headlights and slowly backed out of the drive. I went down the street just a bit farther, then pulled over and called Mike.

"Hey, Tess, what's up?"

"I just arrived at Tony's. There is a car in his driveway. It looks like it might be the one the man who shot Star was driving."

"Are you sure?"

"Not at all. It could belong to a friend of Tony's, and nothing at all might be wrong. But my gut tells me otherwise. What should I do?"

"Where are you?"

"Parked along the street near Tony's place."

"Stay there. I'm on my way."

I hung up and forced down the nausea that had begun to bubble up as I waited. Even if Mike used his siren and lights, it was going to take him a good fifteen minutes to get up the mountain. I couldn't just sit here doing nothing. Could I? What if Tony had been shot? What if there was still time to save him? The man who'd shot Star hadn't hesitated at all. For all I knew, Tony was already dead.

I couldn't wait another minute; I got out of the car and started toward the house. I had to walk carefully so as not to trip as I tromped through the woods, which were covered with the four feet of snow we'd gotten on Friday night. Of course, the snow had settled somewhat, but it was still a lot deeper than I'd like to have to walk through. I didn't know what I was going to do when I got to the house. I didn't have a weapon, so charging in wasn't going to help anyone, but if Tony was in trouble, I couldn't just do nothing. I'd left Tilly in the Jeep, which she wasn't happy about, but if I ended up getting shot, I didn't want her in harm's way.

I approached the house from the back. When I was close enough to get a peek through a window, I made my way toward a low window as silently as I could. A quick peek in the window showed an empty room. I continued on to the next window and the next, trying to figure out where Tony was. A peek into the living room revealed that Tang and Tinder were safely sleeping on the sofa. I continued around to find Titan locked up in the small room Tony mainly used for extra storage. Well, that wasn't good. If Titan was locked away, Tony was definitely in trouble. I didn't see him, nor did I see the driver of the blue car, but chances were whoever was in the house with Tony was in the computer room, a basement room that, of course, had no windows.

I made my way around to the back door and was preparing to penetrate the interior when I felt a hand clamp firmly over my mouth.

My instinct was to scream, but given the fact that I could barely breathe, I resisted.

"I'm going to remove my hand," said a voice behind me. "Don't scream."

I nodded. The hand fell away, and I turned around. "Dad?"

He looked at me, hugged me hard and fast, and then stepped back.

"What are you doing here?"

"Trying to prevent that boyfriend of yours from getting himself killed. I don't know the layout of the house. Where do you think they are?"

"In the computer room. It is built into the center of the basement. It is a secure cleanroom, so the only access is the door. How did you know Tony was in trouble?"

"I've been tracking Norlander ever since I heard about Star. He won't hesitate to kill Tony once he gives him whatever he wants."

"You think he is here to dig up information on you?"

"That is the only reason I can think of for Tony not to be already dead. I'm going in. You wait here."

"But…"

"No buts. Stay here. If I have to worry about you, I can't do my job."

I wanted to argue, but I didn't. I watched as my dad headed around the house. I was more terrified than I could possibly describe, but somehow I knew in my heart that my daddy would save the day. Saving the day was, after all, the things dads did. I knew Mike was on the way and wanted to warn him, so I stepped away from the house and called him.

"Dad is here," I blurted out when Mike answered.

"What?"

"He went in to save Tony. He said to wait outside."

"Where are you?"

"At the back of the house. Near the back door."

"I thought I told you to wait in the Jeep."

"You did. I didn't. I'm sorry. If you are close, you need to be quiet, so you don't alert anyone inside that you are here. Turn off the sirens and park on the street. I'll meet you at the front of the house."

Mike paused before he answered. "Okay. Meet me by the woodshed. I'll be there in less than a minute."

The next few minutes were some of the worst of my life. Mike showed up, and we talked about what to do. He was determined to go inside and do what he could to moderate the situation. I supposed I didn't blame him, but Dad had said to wait. Of course, he told me to wait; I was unarmed and untrained. But he might actually welcome Mike's help. After a brief discussion, Mike told me to stay where I was, and he headed toward the house.

I hated waiting under the best of circumstances. This was unbearable. I found myself listening for a gunshot. Although if there was a gunshot inside the secure room, I wouldn't be able to hear it; the room was soundproof as well as air-tight. I wondered if Mike had called for backup or if it was just him and Dad. It seemed like it had been hours since Mike had gone in, but in reality, it had probably been less than five minutes from the time he left me to the time I saw the front door open. I held my breath as I waited to see who came out and then began to sob tears of joy when I saw Mike walk out with Tony right behind him.

I ran toward the house and threw myself into Tony's arms. "Oh, God, I was so scared."

"I know. Me too." He tightened his grip around me.

"Norlander?" I asked.

"Dead," Tony said. "Your dad shot him just as he was pulling the trigger to shoot Mike."

I looked around. "Where's Dad?"

"He went out the back," Tony informed me.

"But why?" It was at that moment that Mike's backup pulled into Tony's drive.

"I think that is why," Tony said.

I supposed that made sense. I noticed that it wasn't only Frank responding, but there was also a man in a black sedan who looked very official. I supposed this was Mike's FBI buddy. I wasn't aware he was in town, but Mike did say he was looking into things.

The next several hours were somewhat of a blur. I went and got Tilly, and then Tony and I were interviewed by both Mike and his FBI friend. By the time Frank and the FBI guy left, I was physically and emotionally exhausted. Norlander's body had been removed from Tony's house. I could see that Mike was upset that the man had died. If he'd lived, he might have been able to get something out of him. Still, I was sure that Dad had done what he'd needed to do to save Mike's life.

"Did you see him?" I asked Mike when it was just the three of us.

"Briefly."

"Did you speak to him?"

He nodded. "I came up behind him. He motioned for me to be quiet and cover his left side, which I did. I went in, Norlander aimed his gun at me, shots were fired, and the next thing I knew, Norlander was dead. I turned around to say something to Dad, but he was already gone. I didn't even see him leave, but Tony saw him duck out the back door as soon as Norlander was down and the situation was contained. I wish he would have waited. I have so many questions for him."

I put my arms around Mike and gave him a hard hug. "I know. Me too. I just think that this is one of those instances when the answers we need are going to take time."

Chapter 20

Tuesday, December 24

Tony and I never did get our romantic dinner last night, but I was happy to be with my family tonight. Having just seen Dad, if only for a minute, left me feeling a deep sense of loss I hadn't experienced since those first dark days after Mom had been told about the accident. I knew that the man I remembered as my father was only an illusion he'd created, and the more I got to know about the man that he really was, the more I realized that I'd never actually known him at all. But that didn't mean I didn't *want* to know him. I'd struggled with the whole thing and wondered many times whether he was a good guy or a bad guy, but after saving Tony's life, I knew that he'd always be good in my book.

"Heck of a couple of days," Mike said into my ear as he hugged me and kissed me on the cheek.

"Tell me about it."

"Have you seen or heard from Dad?"

"No. You?" I asked.

"No."

I could see that Mike was both saddened and deeply affected by the encounter. I knew exactly how he felt. "I think he is long gone by now. He only seems to show up when he has a really good reason for doing so. I'd love to be able to spend time with him, but to be honest, I'm not sure whether we'll ever see him again."

Mike hung his head. I hated that he looked so sad. "If he does contact you, will you let me know?" he asked.

"I will. I promise. From now on, we really are in this together."

Mike hugged me again and then went to join Bree. Mike, Tony, Bree, and I were all pretty stressed over everything that had happened, but we'd decided not to fill Mom in on it at least right now. With the events in town for which she had been responsible behind her, she seemed downright giddy with relief and had expressed enough joy and happiness for all of us.

"Did you ever find the deed that the woman you arrested said had been left in that old desk?" Mom asked Mike when she emerged from the kitchen to join us in the living room.

"Yes, we did find the deed and all the other items from the desk," Mike answered. "On the night that Bree, Tess, Tony, and I searched Colton's house, Tess found two sets of numbers and letters written on a notepad in his nightstand. It took me a while to figure out the significance of those numbers and letters, but as it turns out, they were related to a safety deposit box that Colton had opened in a bank in Billings. The first set was the box's number, and the second was the code to get into it."

"Why go all the way to Billings?" Mom wondered.

"We don't know for sure, and Colton isn't here for us to ask," Mike began, "but he opened the box the day after Star was shot. I think Colton suspected that her death might be connected to the desk and the items they found in it, and he felt he needed to hide everything until he could figure out what to do with it, so he opened a safety deposit box where he believed no one would think to look for it."

"But why didn't he go to you for help if he suspected that Star had been shot because of the things they found in the desk?" Mom asked. "It seems he would have wanted to not only protect himself but to help you to track down Star's killer."

Mike slowly shook his head. "I have no idea."

Mike glanced at me, and I nodded slightly. He and I had already discussed the items he found in the safety deposit box in Billings. The file that Denton's friend had sent to Star was not among the things he'd stored in the box, but we now knew that Norlander had shot both Star and Colton. We'd strongly suspected that Colton had been in possession of the file at some point. Otherwise, why would he even have been on Norlander's radar? The problem was, we had no idea what had become of the file after Colton had it or what sort of information it contained. But I supposed that answering those questions were tasks for another day.

"This whole thing is just too confusing," Mom said. "First Star and Colton bought a desk with a secret compartment that holds important papers, and then both of them were shot and killed. It seems logical that they died because of the contents of the desk, but as it turns out, it was just some random guy who murdered them. Why?"

I looked at Mike and decided to let him answer. We weren't ready to tell Mom about Dad or any of the circumstances of his faked death, so we couldn't explain who Norlander was or why he shot Star and Colton. In reality, we could only speculate that he shot them because of what they knew, and even that was speculation.

"We don't have all the details, and the man is dead," Mike said. "It may just have to be enough to know that the man responsible for the deaths has been brought to justice."

"I guess so," Mom said. "Dinner should be ready in about fifteen minutes. I'm going to head into the kitchen to see to the final preparations."

"Can I help?" I asked.

"No. You kids just relax. I'll give a holler when I'm ready for you to come into the dining room."

As soon as Mom left, I grabbed Mike to ask him about the prints on the open/closed sign in Star's shop. We'd already pretty much determined that the person who kicked Jillian out of the store that day wasn't Norlander.

"The prints on the sign, which we assume belong to the man who visited Star's shop the day Jillian Brown was there, belong to someone named Omar Devonshire. Like Norlander, Devonshire once worked for Henderson."

"'Once worked'?" I asked.

"According to the information I was able to pull up, Omar Devonshire died three years ago."

I rolled my eyes. "What is it with all the faked deaths? It almost seems trendy at this point."

"I agree," Mike said. "I spoke to Tony about it, and we both feel that Omar Devonshire is likely to pop up again. I guess all we can do is keep an eye out for him."

"So, is this the same man who came out to Tony's house to warn him away from looking for Dad, and the same man who pulled you out of a restaurant to give you the same warning?"

"Tony and I both think so," Mike answered. "If I had to guess, he is working for, or at least with, and not against Dad. We think the guy is trying to keep Dad off everyone's radar."

I'd had enough espionage for one evening and said as much. Mike agreed, and, grabbing Tony by the arm, they headed toward the liquor cabinet.

"Do you want a drink?" I asked Bree, intending to join them at the cabinet.

"No." She leaned in close to me. "Mike and I haven't told anyone this yet, but we're trying for a baby."

My brows shot up. "Wow. That is so great." I leaned in and hugged her. "How long have you been trying?"

"A month. I was going to tell you right away, but then we had the fight. I'm glad that we made up. It was really hard on me, not having anyone to tell my secrets to."

I hugged Bree again. "Me too. Let's not ever fight again. No matter what. We'll just talk it out." I supposed that deep inside, I knew that the fight between us would not be our last, but in this moment, I was as happy to have my best friend back as she was to have someone to tell her secrets to. "Have you told anyone else?"

"No. And we don't plan to. Well, maybe Tony. I don't want to tell your mother or anyone in my family. Not that I don't love your mom and my family, but I don't want everyone asking me how it is going every time we see them."

"I get that." And I did. I could totally see my mom going grandma crazy with the news, which would lead her to become way overinvolved. "Mom has been bugging Mike about a baby since before you were even married. It's a smart move to wait to tell her until after you are actually expecting."

"I'm glad you understand. I'm both excited and terrified about what the next year will bring. I don't need the extra stress of everyone watching and waiting for me to conceive like I am the proverbial pot of boiling water."

"I get why you would be excited about the upcoming year, but why terrified?"

Bree shrugged. "I don't know. I want a baby more than anything, but something deep down inside is warning me that the road might not be as easy as I hope. What if we can't conceive? What if we do conceive, but there is something wrong with the baby? There are just so many unknowns."

I took Bree's hand in mine. "There are, but you aren't in this alone. You have Mike, and you have Tony and me. Whatever happens, we'll go through it together."

Bree hugged me again. I could tell she was crying, but that was okay because bearing the tears of those you love is part of being a family, and having a family who loves you is the most important thing in the world.

Chapter 21

"What a great night," I said to Tony as we drove back to my cabin, where Tilly and the other animals were waiting.

"It was an exceptional Christmas Eve, and it's not over yet," Tony said.

"It's not?" I yawned.

"We never had our couple's night last night, so I prepared a few surprises for you."

I smiled. "You did? Like what?"

He took my hand in his and rested our joined hands on the seat between us. "You'll have to wait until we get home to find out."

"I can't wait."

"Oh, I think you can." Tony winked at me.

He had left the exterior lights on, so when we pulled up to the cabin, it looked like a Christmas village. He parked and then ran around to my side of the truck and lifted me into his arms. When he began to carry me toward the front door, I started to laugh.

"Carrying someone across the threshold is a marriage thing, not a Christmas thing."

"I know."

He set me down when we arrived at the door. He took out his key and swung the door open. The first thing I noticed after the animals all greeted us was a pile of presents under the tree. The second thing was the angel atop the tree. I frowned. "I thought you understood about the angel."

Tony didn't answer, so I turned to look at him. He was frowning.

"Tony?"

"The presents are from me, and I have a fire ready to light, and champagne chilling in the refrigerator, and even a very decadent chocolate dessert, but I promise that I had nothing to do with the angel."

"But…" I looked at the tree again, and in that moment, I knew. "Dad." Tears streamed down my face as the truth of where the angel had come from gripped me. He must have stopped by while we were out.

"Tess?" Tony asked. "Are you okay?"

I couldn't quite manage words just then, so I simply nodded. The idea that Dad had thought of me on Christmas after all these years was almost more than I could process. I had no idea how he knew when we'd be out, but in my heart, I knew that the angel was a message to me that although we couldn't be together, he still loved me.

I stepped toward the tree as my phone buzzed. It was Mike. "You'll never guess what I found when Bree and I got home."

Next from Kathi Daley Books

Preview:

Twas a week before Christmas and all through the inn... I paused and smiled at my computer screen. I'd been trying to work on the thriller that was due to my editor in less than two months, but all I'd come up with were meaningless phrases that seemed to pop in my head as huge snowflakes drifted gently to the ground outside my window. I had to admit that when combined with the scent of evergreen from the bushy fir in the corner of my bedroom, the bright red bows I'd tied to my bedposts, and the gentle snoring generated by my Maine Coon cat, Rufus, as he slept soundly on my pillow, the setting really was quite magical.

"How about some background music?" I said to my dog, Molly, who was laying on a dog pillow next to my feet. She thumped her tail in agreement as I turned on the radio to the gentle lyrics of *O Holy Night*. The popular carol generated feelings of nostalgia, which caused me to lean back in my chair, close my eyes, and really embrace the perfection of the moment. Taking a deep breath, I allowed my thoughts to turn to the cookies my best friend and roommate, Georgia Carter, was baking in the kitchen. In addition to being the manager of the inn I'd purchased on a whim just over a year ago, she was a heck of a good cook and baker. Her reputation for original and creative dishes had earned her a place in a Christmas cookie contest that was going to be aired on local cable during the Christmas Eve edition of the popular show *Coastal Maine Living*. The competition was open to entrants across the country, so being chosen as a contestant in the final round was actually a really big thing, and Georgia had been trying out new recipes for weeks.

After a moment of blissful serenity, I opened my eyes and looked back toward the computer screen. I exited the page where I'd been doodling thoughts of Christmas past, present, and future, and returned my attention to my work in progress. I had to admit if only to myself, that I really didn't have much. The title page was pretty awesome: *Currents from the Past* by New York Times Bestselling Author Abagail Sullivan.

I smiled once again. I loved being a writer and really wouldn't give it up for any other profession, but I had to wonder if my decision to leave the romance genre for books that were classified as thriller and suspense hadn't been a mistake. Given my total lack of usable words in spite of the hours I'd spent sitting at my computer, I was fairly certain my doubt as to the direction my career had taken was justified. The last thriller I'd published had been a huge success, and I knew I should ride that wave, but somehow writing about serial killers and husbands with deep dark secrets didn't fill the space in my soul the way writing about family, holidays, best friends, and the perfect guy once had.

Maybe I needed to step away from my career and think about a change. Of course, *Currents from the*

Past was under contract, so I did have that to deal with.

I might not be able to shelve my work in progress and write the story my soul was yearning to write at this very minute, but I could take a break and see if Georgia needed a taste tester for her latest creation. Having different types of cookies to taste each day had been a lot of fun and oh so delicious, but I supposed if I didn't get up out of my chair and get some exercise, I'd end December ten pounds heavier than I'd started the month.

"Oh, good," Georgia said as I emerged from the bedroom, which also served as my office. "I'm ready for today's tasting."

"You know I'm here for you," I smiled.

She passed me a tray. "These are chocolate pralines. They are really more of a candy, but I modified the recipe somewhat so they would qualify as a cookie."

I took a bite. "They're delicious. Are those hazelnuts I taste?"

Georgia grinned and nodded. "There are hazelnuts in the recipe, along with fine oats, gingerbread spice, three types of chocolate, and a lot of other good quality ingredients."

"I really like them." I took another bite. "A lot. I'm not sure if I like these or the creamy caramel and pecan cookies you made yesterday better. Of course, the cherry fizz delights you made the day before that were delicious as well. In fact, everything you've tried has been so wonderful that I'm not sure how you will choose which recipe to enter in the contest."

Georgia washed her hands and then dried them on a Christmas towel. The kitchen in the cottage, like the rest of the cottage where Georgia and I lived, had received the full holiday treatment. "I'm having the guests at the inn taste the cookies I make while they are with us. Then before they leave, I ask them to rank the cookies they've tasted. So far, everyone has been happy to help out. I know that folks have favorites, based on their own personal tastes, but I'm hoping that in the end, the best recipe will win out. And even if I don't get the feedback I'm hoping for, I think the guests enjoy the extra treats and the opportunity to be involved."

"I bet they do. Taste testing your recipes is indeed a sweet gig." I popped the final bite of my cookie into my mouth.

"Jeremy and Annabelle have been providing their input as well, which really helps on those days we don't have guests. I think Jeremy liked the double fudge chocolates I baked last week, and Annabelle is still talking about the peppermint creams."

Jeremy Slater worked at the inn and lived in the converted basement, along with his eight-year-old niece, Annabelle, who was living with Jeremy while her mother was working overseas. Jeremy took care of the heavy work required to keep the inn running, such as snow removal, yard maintenance, and general repairs, while Georgia acted as the inn manager, head cook, and marketing guru.

"Speaking of guests," I said after a brief pause. "I remember seeing we have a whole new group checking in this week. Will they be with us through the holiday?"

Georgia nodded. "If you remember, we discussed the fact that it would be easier and more relaxing to have long-term guests over the Christmas holiday rather than guests checking in and out every day, so I experimented with a seven day minimum over Christmas."

"And did you get many takers?"

"Actually, I did. In fact, all of the guests who will be with us for Christmas Eve and Christmas Day will be with us for between seven and fourteen days. The first of these long-term guests will be checking in tomorrow."

That did sound good. I'd found that our guests quickly became family, and it would be nice to have a bit more consistency over the holiday. "So, who do we have checking in this week?"

Georgia began putting food away while I grabbed a second cookie. I figured if I gained too much weight and needed to diet, that I could get to it once January rolled around. "The first of our Christmas arrivals is a woman named Mylie Sanders. Mylie is checking in tomorrow and will be with us for a full fourteen days. She is coming to Holiday Bay to meet her soulmate."

"Soulmate?"

Georgia began filling the sink with sudsy water. "Mylie recently turned thirty, which I think got her biological clock ticking. When she made the reservation, she told me that a psychic told her that if she spent Christmas in Holiday Bay, she would meet her one true love. She wasn't sure exactly how long she needed to be here, so she decided on two weeks."

"So, she thinks she will meet her one true love here at the inn?" I clarified.

Georgia answered. "She wasn't really sure if she would meet the man of her dreams here at the inn, or if she'd meet him in town, but the psychic did suggest that she stay at the inn, so she booked a room. As I mentioned, she checks in tomorrow, and will be with us through New Year's."

"I can't wait to meet Mylie. She sounds like an interesting woman."

"We actually spoke on the phone for quite a while," Georgia said. "She seemed cheerful and energetic, and I really think she'll be a fun individual to get to know. And with the added mystery of the man the psychic predicted, I'm sure her stay will be entertaining for all of us."

I broke off a corner of the cookie. "Do we have any single men of comparable age staying with us at the same time that Mylie will be here?"

"Three," Georgia answered. "Which, if you think about it, is pretty unusual. So far, single men in their thirties have not really been our target clientele, although admittedly, we have had a few thirtyish men who have stayed with us while they were in town for reasons related to jobs."

"Such as Ryan Steadman when he was here to interview at the bank and Noah Daniels while he was here for his job interview for the church."

"Exactly."

"So, who are the three lucky bachelors who will be staying with us this month?" I asked.

"Riley Camden is checking in on Friday and will also be here through New Year's," Georgia answered. "He is thirty-two, single, and in town to do a story on the seasonal offerings that can be found in Holiday Bay and the surrounding area."

"So, he's a travel writer?"

She nodded. "He writes a travel blog. I checked it out, and it's really rather good, and it has a huge audience. Riley's blog is a weekly offering with over a hundred thousand followers. I'm hoping to convince him to give the inn a shout out at some point during his stay. I figure that a shout out in a blog with that sort of circulation could really boost our reservations. Especially if we can get him to include photos and a schedule of special events."

I reached down and picked up a bright red ornament that one of the animals had knocked off the tree and had rolled across the room. "That would be fantastic. Especially if he will publish the event schedule. And I agree that if Riley has a nice time with us and he writes about his experience during his stay, the added publicity could really help us. Let's be sure to give him the VIP treatment."

Georgia giggled. "I give everyone the VIP treatment."

I supposed she did. In many ways, Georgia was more like an Inn Mother than a mere manager. "So, who are Mylie's other two potential suitors?"

"Andrew Madison. He is a thirty-four-year-old forensic accountant who will be in town to visit his great aunt. He checks in on Sunday and will be with us through December twenty-ninth. I guess Andrew spent quite a bit of time here in Holiday Bay as a child since his parents traveled extensively. During those times when his parents were away touring the world, Andrew would come to Holiday Bay and stay with his aunt. When we spoke on the phone, he mentioned that those childhood summers are some of the best times in his life."

"A career as a forensic accountant seems both interesting and impressive," I commented. "And I love the fact that he is in town to spend the holiday with his aunt. He sounds like he would make a good husband."

"That's what I thought when I spoke to him. Of course, Mylie isn't here just to find a husband. She is here to find her soulmate. I'm not sure exactly how one is to determine who is and who is not a soulmate, but I imagine that Mylie is looking for a deeper relationship than just a vacation fling."

"Based on what you've said, I'm sure that's true." I got up, replaced the ornament on the tree, and then I headed to the refrigerator for a glass of milk to go with the rest of my cookie. "So, who is bachelor number three?"

"Mark Westgate. Mark is checking in on Saturday and will be with us through December twenty-seventh. He is a successful developer who will be in town to purchase a piece of property where he hopes to build a high-end resort over the next two years. He is single, although based on what I've dug up, it seems he is single because he is married to his job. Still, he appears to be smart, and according to the photo on his website, he is also very good looking. He may be too much of a workaholic for Mylie, but at thirty-eight, he might be feeling ready to settle down. I spoke to Lacy about it, and she actually thinks Mark is a good candidate."

Lacy Parker was a good friend and the wife of my contractor, Lonnie Parker. The couple had six children who I adored.

"Anyone else with theories as to Mylie's perfect match at this point?" I wondered.

Georgia dipped her hands into the sink full of sudsy water. "Jeremy thinks that she'll end up going for someone gorgeous like Riley, and Nikki has voiced her opinion that she will probably go for a guy like Andrew, who seems settled and dependable." Nikki Peyton was our neighbor, and Georgia's boyfriend, Tanner Peyton's, younger sister. She worked part-time at the inn, helping out with the laundry and cleaning.

"And what do you think?" I asked.

"I think that someone like Riley seems the most interesting. Although it sounds as if Mylie is looking for settled and not interesting."

"I would agree with that. So, it sounds like Mylie and her bachelors will occupy four of the six rooms. Who will be occupying the other two?"

"Christy and Haley Baldwin will be in the attic room," Georgia answered. "I wasn't sure we'd be able to fit her in, but I had a few cancellations, and I juggled things around so that we can accommodate her for her entire stay in Holiday Bay."

I found myself smiling. "I'm so glad it worked for Christy and Haley to be with us. I've really missed them." Christy was a widow, who had brought her daughter, Haley, to Holiday Bay last month to spend Thanksgiving with her deceased husband's parents. During her stay over Thanksgiving, we'd discussed the fact that her in-laws wanted her to move to Holiday Bay where they could help out, but Christy had reservations due mostly to the fact that she feared her in-laws might try to take over her life as well as Haley's if they lived in such close proximity. Christy wanted her daughter to know her father's parents, but at what cost? Although Christy did have an added incentive to make the move. During her stay in November, she'd met Noah Daniels who'd been staying at the inn, while in town to interview for the position as the new pastor for the community's church. He'd taken the job and had settled into his new home in town. During the time both guests were at the inn, it seemed that Noah and Christy had really hit it off, and, in my opinion, if they had the opportunity to spend more time together, they might even end up making a connection of the romantic kind.

"I spoke to Christy at length yesterday," Georgia informed me as she bent down to greet Molly, who had wandered out of the bedroom. Molly offered her a paw and was rewarded with a piece of a homemade dog cookie Georgia kept on hand. Of course, that had her Newfoundland, Ramos, lumbering over from his place in front of the fire as well. "She and Haley are both very excited about coming to Holiday Bay for Christmas, and they are extra excited that they are going to be able to spend the entire two weeks with us. They arrive on December nineteenth, and will be with us until January second."

"And the sixth room?" I asked.

"Ben and Beth Trenton. I'm afraid their story is a bit sadder. They lost their only son in Afghanistan last year and didn't want to stay home where they would be reminded of him at every turn, yet they also didn't want to skip Christmas, so they decided on a holiday at the coast. They saw our ad and thought the inn would be a perfect place to nurse their broken hearts. They will be with us for just one week and will check in on December twenty-third."

Now my heart was breaking. I knew what it was like to lose a child. I'd lost my infant son two years ago, so I understood how devastated they must feel. I had to give them credit for not just taking to their bed and pulling the blankets over their heads until January. That is exactly what I'd done that first year. "We'll be sure they have a special holiday that honors their son and creates a space in their hearts for healing."

Georgia smiled warmly at me. "That is one of the reasons why I adore you. You seem to know exactly what to say."

"I might be good with words, but you are good with people." I drank the last of my milk. "You know, I am really looking forward to the holiday this year, and I can't wait to meet Mylie. She sounds like just the sort of person to bring the spirit of the holiday to the inn."

"I agree. When I spoke to her on the phone, I just knew she was going to fit right in. She even seemed excited about the ornament decorating and the other preholiday events we have planned."

"I'm pretty excited about the events we have planned as well. And the inn feels just right with all the decorating you and Jeremy have done."

"We really tried to create a Norman Rockwell moment."

"Did the wreath we ordered for the inn's front door ever show up?" I asked.

She shook her head. "No, but I got an email yesterday that said it would be delivered before five today. I left instructions for the delivery guy to come around to the cottage since I knew we were going to be between guests for a few days, and I wanted to use the kitchen here to practice for the cookie bakeoff."

I glanced out the window at the falling snow. "I hadn't realized the inn was going to be totally empty between guests."

"Initially, I didn't think we'd have a break either, but the last of the weekend guests checked out yesterday, and, the first of the Christmas guests won't check in until tomorrow. At first, I was sorry that we weren't booked straight through December as I thought at one point we would be, but then I realized that with the place empty for a day, we could really get in there and do some deep cleaning. I spoke to Nikki, and she is coming in after her job at the diner, and Jeremy plans to help out once he gets home from picking up Annabelle after pageant rehearsal. I'm going to finish up here and meet them over there."

"I'll help," I offered. I didn't usually participate in the chores or the management of the inn, but I needed a break from writing, and mopping floors and washing windows seemed like as good a diversion as anything. "I'll call Colt and see if he wants to bring pizza by for everyone who will be working this evening."

"Is Colt planning to come by?" Georgia asked about Colt Wider, the man who had become one of my very best friends and provided law enforcement for the town.

"He mentioned that he might. He is going to be leaving to take his niece and nephew to Disney World for a few days and wanted to see me before he left."

Colt's sister and her husband had been killed in a car accident not long before I moved to Holiday Bay, and while their children lived with Colt's parents, their grandparents, he did what he could to help out during the summers and school holidays.

"That sounds like fun. Will he be back by Christmas?"

I nodded. "They leave tomorrow and will be back late in the day on the twenty-third. He is taking the kids to his parents for Christmas, however, so I doubt I'll see him until he gets back from there. I think he plans to drive home on the twenty-sixth or twenty-seventh."

"I'm sorry he won't be here for Christmas, but I do understand him wanting to be with his family."

"He is actually off until after the first, so he plans to spend New Year's Eve and New Year's Day with us. I know we'll have a full inn, but I thought it would be fun to have an early gathering for the guests here at the inn, and then we can migrate to Tanner's and spend New Year's Eve with friends. I asked him about it when I saw him a few days ago, and he seemed to be all for it."

"That sounds fun," Georgia agreed. "I know Tanner is planning a big blowout this year and has even invited some of his trainers to ring in the New Year at his place."

Tanner owned Peyton Academy, a training facility for search and rescue and service dogs.

I glanced out the window. The snow was still coming down at a steady rate. The outdoor lights that Jeremy had strung along the eaves and around the windows of both the inn and the cottage provided a cheery feel to an otherwise dark day. Georgia had added lights to the shrubs and small trees as well, so the entire estate really did feel like a fairyland.

"It looks like a delivery truck is in the drive," I said.

"Oh, good. That should be the wreath for the inn's front door. When I'd ordered a custom wreath made from fresh greenery, I had no idea it would take so long for it to get here." Georgia pulled her jacket on, opened the door, and stepped onto the wrap-around deck. Once the truck stopped, she walked over and spoke to the driver. After a moment, she came back to the cottage. "The driver has the wreath, but he has something else as well."

"Oh, what is it?" I asked.

"A life-size nutcracker. Apparently, it is a gift from Lonnie and Lacy."

I smiled. "I wonder if it's the nutcracker we saw at the antique store a few weeks ago." I'd admired it, but after much deliberation, I'd decided it was too expensive and that I needed to tighten my belt a bit, so I hadn't bought it. "I guess Lacy must have bought it for me. She did make up that excuse to go back to the store after we'd all left. She'd said she'd left her mittens inside, but I had a feeling she was up to something."

"I know Lonnie and Lacy wanted to get you a special gift," Georgia said. "On many occasions, they both voiced how much it meant to them that you trusted Lonnie with the remodel on the inn."

"He did an excellent job. It is I who should be looking for a special gift for them, but I am pretty happy about the gift they bought for me."

"The delivery guy wants to know what to do with it. He has a handcart and is willing to bring it inside. It's made of wood and close to six feet tall, so he says it is heavy."

"Let's put it in front of the window next to the fireplace in the parlor," I answered. "That way, everyone can enjoy it, it won't be in the way of normal traffic patterns, and we won't have to lug it upstairs."

She nodded. "Sounds good. I'll show the guy where to take it."

"I'll pull on my boots and meet you over there."

I was going to have to call Lacy with a huge thank you. The nutcracker really was exquisite. It was really old and in excellent condition. I supposed it was somewhat impractical since it would be hard to move around, and I would need to find a place to store it for eleven months out of the year, but from the moment I saw it, I wanted it."

"So, what do you think?" Georgia asked, taking a step back once the delivery driver had positioned the tall statue where I'd indicated.

The tall figure provided just the right accent to top off the room. "I think it's perfect." I handed the driver an envelope with a generous tip. "Thank you so much for bringing it in. I'm not sure how we would have managed without you."

"No problem. Merry Christmas." With that, the man left.

I turned to Georgia. "Isn't he great?"

"I think it's perfect. It gives the entire room personality. I wonder how old it actually is."

"The woman at the antique store told us that she was certain it was more than fifty years old, but she wasn't sure of the exact age." I smiled as I really took it in. "I think our nutcracker is going to make a wonderful conversation starter."

"I agree. There is something about the statue that just seems to scream the fact that if he could speak, he'd have an interesting story to tell."

Georgia looked up, as did I at the sound of the door opening and then closing, followed by footsteps on the hardwood floor.

"Hey, guys, what's going on?" Nikki asked, after poking her head in through the door and then joining us in the parlor.

"Lonnie and Lacy sent us this life-size nutcracker," I answered.

"Awesome." She stepped forward for a better look. "Annabelle is going to love it. She was just telling me the other day that she'd gone to see *The Nutcracker* with her mother last Christmas, and how it had turned out to be one of the best days they'd spent together."

"It is sad that her mother couldn't make it home this year," I commented.

Nikki nodded. "It is, but Annabelle seems to be having fun with Hannah." Nikki was referring to Annabelle's best friend, Hannah Danson. "And I know she is excited to be part of the Holiday Bay Christmas Pageant. She has been talking nonstop about it since she was cast as the snow princess."

"She has seemed excited about the part," I agreed.

"And we are planning a lot of activities between now and Christmas that an eight-year-old will enjoy," Nikki added. "I'm sure we can keep her occupied."

"We can, and Jeremy is really good with her. He'll make sure she has the perfect Christmas in spite of the fact that her mother isn't here." As I said it, I was determined to make sure Annabelle's Christmas was the best we could provide.

Georgia walked over to the window and looked out. "The snow is coming down harder."

"I noticed that," I answered. "The weather report is calling for clearing overnight. I'm hoping it is clear this weekend for the sleigh rides and snowman competition we plan to sponsor here at the inn."

"I think the forecast is for a mild weekend. If it does snow, we'll focus on wreath making and ornament decorating inside."

The conversation paused as the front door slammed shut. Must be Annabelle. I'd talked to her about not slamming doors, but she was only eight, and eight-year-olds tended to slam doors.

"Anyone here?" Annabelle called out.

"We're in the parlor," Georgia called back.

I could hear the sound of running feet in the instant before Annabelle appeared in the doorway. "Oh, wow! Look at that." She walked over to the nutcracker and touched his arm. "He is beautiful. Just like the nutcracker in the ballet."

"He is pretty awesome," Jeremy seconded. "Where did you get it?"

"It's a gift from Lonnie and Lacy," I said. "Isn't he great?"

"He really is," Jeremy agreed.

"I love his hat, but the chin strap is covering his mouth. Aren't nutcrackers supposed to have mouths that open and close?"

"The strap from the hat is hiding the nutcracker's mouth, but I checked when he first arrived and confirmed it is there behind the strap," I said.

"I feel like the fact that you can't see his mouth gives him a shifty look," Jeremy said.

"What do you mean?" I asked.

"I'm not sure exactly." He stared at the statue for another minute. "It's something with the eyes. They look guarded. Like he has a secret."

"Maybe he really does come to life at night," Annabelle giggled.

Georgia smiled. "That would be fun. Maybe you can get up in the middle of the night and dance with him."

"And maybe there will be sugarplum fairies." Annabelle twirled around the room.

Having an eight-year-old in the family really did add an element to our lives that I enjoyed. "How was the rehearsal for the pageant?" I asked.

"It was really, really good," Annabelle said after she stopped pirouetting around the room. "The play is on Saturday, and we are going to do a full dress rehearsal on Friday. The director was worried that not everyone knew their lines, but I think everyone does. Are you coming?" She looked around the room. "Are all of you coming?"

"We wouldn't miss it for the world," I confirmed.

"Good. I really want you to see my snow princess costume. It is all silvery and sparkly. It really is the best costume in the whole play."

"What is Hannah going to be?" Georgia asked.

"Actually, she is playing the piano and doesn't really have a costume."

Hannah was Annabelle's best friend and an accomplished concert pianist in spite of her young age.

"She is wearing a red dress with black tights and black shoes," Annabelle added.

"Well, I can't wait to see her all dressed up then," I answered.

"Do we have cookies to taste?" Annabelle asked, seeming to grow bored with the current conversation.

"We do," Georgia said. "Anyone who wants in on the tasting should follow me to the kitchen."

Jeremy, Nikki, and Annabelle all followed Georgia out of the room. I figured the two cookies I'd had should do me through dinner. I adjusted the lights on the tree and then stood back to look at the nutcracker one more time. Jeremy was right. The nutcracker did have shifty eyes, which made him look like he was keeping a secret. I took out my phone, snapped a photo, and sent it off to Lacy. Then I dialed her number. I wanted to thank her and let her know the huge decoration had arrived. The nutcracker really had been a thoughtful and heartfelt, if somewhat impractical gift. I supposed that the logistics of storing him could be an issue, yet he really did seem to add an element to the room that seemed to pull the other decorations together in a special way.

Of course, as we would soon learn, the real magic of the nutcracker was the secret he had kept for more than fifty years. A secret, I was to learn, that would be steeped with both warmth and heartache and would be revealed to us as the week unfolded.

Books by Kathi Daley
Come for the murder, stay for the romance

Zoe Donovan Cozy Mystery:
Halloween Hijinks
The Trouble With Turkeys
Christmas Crazy
Cupid's Curse
Big Bunny Bump-off
Beach Blanket Barbie
Maui Madness
Derby Divas
Haunted Hamlet
Turkeys, Tuxes, and Tabbies
Christmas Cozy
Alaskan Alliance
Matrimony Meltdown
Soul Surrender
Heavenly Honeymoon
Hopscotch Homicide
Ghostly Graveyard
Santa Sleuth
Shamrock Shenanigans
Kitten Kaboodle
Costume Catastrophe
Candy Cane Caper
Holiday Hangover
Easter Escapade
Camp Carter
Trick or Treason
Reindeer Roundup

Hippity Hoppity Homicide
Firework Fiasco
Henderson House
Holiday Hostage
Lunacy Lake
Celtic Christmas – *December 2019*

Zimmerman Academy The New Normal
Zimmerman Academy New Beginnings
Ashton Falls Cozy Cookbook

The Inn at Holiday Bay:
Boxes in the Basement
Letters in the Library
Message in the Mantel
Answers in the Attic
Haunting in the Hallway
Pilgrim in the Parlor
Note in the Nutcracker
Blizzard in the Bay – *January 2020*

A Cat in the Attic Mystery:
The Curse of Hollister House
The Mystery before Christmas
   e Case of the Cupid Caper – *January 2020*

ıles and Tails Cozy Mystery:
  ⁊ and Juliet
    ⁊atter
     ırry Tail
       ʰout Felines
         ʰy Hollow
           ʾ Past

A Tale of Two Tabbies
The Great Catsby
Count Catula
The Cat of Christmas Present
A Winter's Tail
The Taming of the Tabby
Frankencat
The Cat of Christmas Future
Farewell to Felines
A Whisker in Time
The Catsgiving Feast
A Whale of a Tail
The Catnap Before Christmas
A Mew Beginning – *Early 2020*

A Tess and Tilly Mystery:

The Christmas Letter
The Valentine Mystery
The Mother's Day Mishap
The Halloween House
The Thanksgiving Trip
The Saint Paddy's Promise
The Halloween Haunting
The Christmas Clause
The Puppy Project – *Early 2020*

Rescue Alaska Mystery:

Finding Justice
Finding Answers
Finding Courage
Finding Christmas
Finding Shelter – *Early 2020*

The Hathaway Sisters:
Harper
Harlow
Hayden – *Early 2020*

Writers' Retreat Mystery:
First Case
Second Look
Third Strike
Fourth Victim
Fifth Night
Sixth Cabin
Seventh Chapter
Eighth Witness
Ninth Grave

Tj Jensen Paradise Lake Mystery:
Pumpkins in Paradise
Snowmen in Paradise
 ikinis in Paradise
   ristmas in Paradise
     ies in Paradise
      veen in Paradise
       e in Paradise
        s in Paradise
           Paradise
            g in Paradise

by the Sea:
the Sea

Thanksgiving by the Sea

Sand and Sea Hawaiian Mystery:
Murder at Dolphin Bay
Murder at Sunrise Beach
Murder at the Witching Hour
Murder at Christmas
Murder at Turtle Cove
Murder at Water's Edge
Murder at Midnight
Murder at Pope Investigations

Seacliff High Mystery:
The Secret
The Curse
The Relic
The Conspiracy
The Grudge
The Shadow
The Haunting

Road to Christmas Romance:
Road to Christmas Past

USA Today best-selling author Kathi Daley lives in beautiful Lake Tahoe with her husband Ken. When she isn't writing, she likes spending time hiking the miles of desolate trails surrounding her home. She has authored more than a hundred books in eleven series, including Zoe Donovan Cozy Mysteries, Whales and Tails Island Mysteries, Tess and Tilly Cozy Mysteries, A Cat in the Attic Mystery, Sand and Sea Hawaiian Mysteries, Tj Jensen Paradise Lake Series, Inn at Holiday Bay Cozy Mysteries, Writers' Retreat Southern Seashore Mysteries, Rescue Alaska Paranormal Mysteries, Haunting by the Sea Paranormal Mysteries, Family Ties Mystery Romances, and Seacliff High Teen Mysteries. Find out more about her books at www.kathidaley.com

Stay up-to-date:
Newsletter, *The Daley Weekly* http://eepurl.com/NRPDf
Webpage – www.kathidaley.com
Facebook at Kathi Daley Books –
www.facebook.com/kathidaleybooks
Kathi Daley Books Group Page –
https://www.facebook.com/groups/569578823146850/
E-mail – kathidaley@kathidaley.com
Twitter at Kathi Daley@kathidaley –
https://twitter.com/kathidaley
Amazon Author Page –
https://www.amazon.com/author/kathidaley
BookBub – https://www.bookbub.com/authors/kathi-daley

Made in the USA
Coppell, TX
06 December 2019

12456795R00118